Evolution of a

Species

I0612642

By

David Grother II

Evolution of a Species

By

David Grother II

Published by Alternative Book Press

Copyright © 2016 David Grother II

ISBN-13: 978-1-940122-34-2

Published by Alternative Book Press

Chapter 1

The wind outside was whipping in all directions in the cold colorless morning, breaking against the stone and metal of the dimly lit structure. Surrounded by the blankets of snow, it was a little oasis of darkness out in the desolate frozen plains of Russia. An old prison, the structure had slipped its proprietors' minds, leaving it behind for time to take care of. However, regardless of the lack of conveniences, such as electrical heating, and as cold as it was in his small cell, Abraham didn't feel the least bit uncomfortable. A certain numbness had gradually taken over his mind and body after more than a decade of living in one of the worst prisons Russia had to offer out of all 46 of its provinces. Had his offense been different, it's possible that he would have ended up somewhere else, but that no longer mattered.

The days and weeks had blended together giving his time there a surreal feeling. The cells at the prison were numerous and isolated, each containing the necessities for living, making it easier on the guards, who now only took the prisoners out of the cell for hygienic purposes. It used to be that once or twice a year a couple prisoners at a time would be let out into the yard for an hour, but even then most just kept to themselves after so long of only having themselves for company, due to the solidarity that was forced upon them. Eventually, the guards gave it up seeing that most prisoners would rather stay in their cell then face the outside world, and only feel a longing that was difficult to get rid of for months afterward.

After the first 2 years, time had lost all meaning for Abraham. All life could have stopped and he wouldn't have thought the least bit about it. He had no hope of ever escaping or being set free and once he'd adjusted to his new life, time died. He was lost inside his mind. He would be lying on his cot one moment and sitting in his lonely wooden chair the next. There was only the moment he was in and nothing else. Visions frequented his mind as well, sending him into a state of terror in most incidents, but occasionally they wouldn't be so bad. Someone to talk to or maybe even an animal, but as time went on his mind became less creative at deterring him from reality, and then eventually they ceased. Dreams, when they came, were more realistic to Abraham than when he was awake. Reliving scenes from his past, or perhaps even something he'd read. The cell was just a bad dream he would wake up to and realize it had never happened. He'd never even been to the prison; he was simply sleeping at his home with his wife, having a horrible nightmare.

Abraham regained consciousness to notice a tall well-kept man was shaving his head with an electric razor. His hair must have grown too long. It crossed his mind for a second, but then he started slipping back into his mindless, dream state. But something caught his eye. A patch of brown hair fell from his head into the path of his vision.

Across the brown patch, there were a few grey hairs scattered throughout. Time returned to Abraham with a grotesque feeling. Had it been that long since he'd been sent here that his hair had begun changing colors? Why couldn't he have just died? The food, the weather, the diseases, or even one of the upset guards could have all killed him. Why did he have to rot? From that day on no matter how hard he tried, he couldn't get back to his mindless, timeless state of bliss. Why he was denied that privilege, he only wished to know, but things weren't the same as they had been.

The days dragged on and the hours were even worse. The only thing Abraham could do was waste time by reading, but even that lost its meaning the last couple years. The stories of religion, adventures, politics, and crime had all lost their interest after being read thirty or more times. The issues in them became unimportant and no longer held any new information that hadn't previously been found. Now Abraham just spent the months lying in his cot, staring at the ceiling. He played his life out in his mind over and over again analyzing his decisions. He had made so many mistakes. Everything in his life could have been different, if only he had been less selfish and negligent. However much he tormented himself about his decisions there was nothing to be done about it.

Even the original feelings Abraham had had about the prison had passed with time. Neither the cold darkness nor his filthy cell bothered him any longer. The bed bugs and the maggots in his food both had also lost their disgusting disposition, but the one thing he could no longer stand was the crying of the newly imprisoned men on his cell block. If they would only cry a little quieter. He couldn't stand hearing someone who still had hope enough for the future, or perhaps even had had a happy enough past to cry about. The only thing that gave Abraham comfort was that soon the men would be educated by the prison. They would learn how the rest of their lives were going to be. Once they had spent a couple months in the prison they would become as passive and distant, or even as insane, as the rest of the inmates. That or they would die. Suicides were as common as death from diseases were.

It must have been near morning because he heard footsteps coming. Most likely one of the guards coming around on patrol, but secretly Abraham hoped that they were coming to take the latest crying inmate away. To his surprise they stopped at his cell and opened the thick metal door, the dim light of the hallway causing Abraham to squint as it slowly entered his cell. "Get up and put your hands on the wall!" one of the three guards who had come shouted forcefully at Abraham, as they piled into his cell, clubs in hand. He slowly sat up on his cot and put his feet to the cold stone floor. He stood up and positioned himself, hands pressed against the cold gritty wall. There was a lot of noise outside in the corridor, which had flowed in as soon as the guards had opened the door. What's going on, Abraham thought curiously. Maybe they were cleaning out and taking some of the old and diseased prisoners to be exterminated. Once an inmate got to a certain age the guards didn't want to take the time to let him deteriorate in his cell so they took him down to the oven. After such an occurrence all the inmates on the man's cell block would have meat in their soupy mash as if it were some sick joke. He'd seen it happen plenty of times before, but the round-ups were never as busy as whatever was going on this day.

They cuffed him, and led him out of the cell block, but to his surprise they took him out into the snowy court yard where a lot of other prisoners were already standing in spaced out rows. He soon noticed that there were guards behind him as well bringing out other prisoners. They lined the prisoners up in rows. Abraham was half paying attention. It had been awhile since he'd been out into the courtyard. It must have been years even. He figured he liked the summers better than the winters, judging from the dull deathly theme the world had taken. It was painfully bright out, the little light there was reflecting off the snow covered ground. It'd been a long time since Abraham had seen snow. Memories from his childhood rushed back to him. Such beauty is contained within snow. The purity of the whiteness, but so easily contaminated. He looked at the patch he was standing on and saw how deformed and discolored the snow under his feet had become. Was it because of him or had the guards or other prisoners stepped on it before him?

More and more prisoners were brought out. Abraham couldn't believe how rugged some of them looked. Did he look this bad? More than half of them didn't have more than a couple of teeth even. Many had dirty tangled facial hair, and had obviously had not had haircuts in quite a while as he had. It was plain to see the toll that the prison was taking on the inmates, mentally as well as physically. The constant whispered conversations some were having with themselves, as well as the obvious anxiety that was being felt from being away from the familiarity of the cell. Abraham's feet were starting to get cold from the snow he was standing on. "Alright, listen up! Mother Russia has decided to give you a second chance. If you choose to fight for her you may win your freedom, if you survive to the wars end. If you accept this opportunity then you'll be shipped out for further physical and mental examination, and training in about two weeks. The one-hundred and ten of you are the ones that I deemed capable enough for now but some of you may be sent back here if you're unable to fight." The Warden was a tall defined man with a thick bushy mustache under his fat red nose. Strong and broad shouldered with a face that fit his proud brutal personality. He was a true Russian.

"When Sgt. Konstantinov comes around with the clip board tell him your name and whether or not you accept."

Tell them his name? Abraham could barely remember his name. It'd been a long time since he was referred to as it, or even referred to himself as it. A smaller man with a clipboard was walking around to each man. This must be Konstantinov. Every man more or less was taking the offer from what Abraham could see, but why would they not? The only choices they had were dying in the war or dying in the cell. Most figured that the war would be faster, so they took the opportunity. Konstantinov stepped up to Abraham.

"Do you understand the offer that the warden has given you and do you accept it?"

"Yes," Abraham said, unfamiliar to the movements of his mouth forming words.

"Name?"

"Abraham Chopiak."

Konstantinov walked onto the next man in line after scribbling Abraham's name down. Abraham looked around. Some of the inmates were smiling, happy that the impossible was happening, but most were just as passive as they were before, probably not even having comprehended what anyone was saying to them and only responding because they were provoked to. Abraham was happy enough, though he didn't show it.

Chapter 2

The next two weeks were the best of Abrahams stay, for no other reason than the quality of food that was given to them; borsht with potatoes, beef, carrots, and tomato. It was the best meal that Abraham could remember ever having.

As the time for them to leave drew closer, a false hope among some of the newer inmates started growing. Some of the prisoners even started exercising in their cells. Abraham had his suspicions but when the day came, the government made good on its word. He and the other prisoners were escorted outside into the retreating winter and put on large buses to take them to the training camp. It'd been too long since most of them had even thought about having a future away from the prison, that the little change that had happened in their lives was overwhelming.

The anxiety and nervousness was visible in their faces, even underneath the dirt and malnourishment.

Everyone boarded the buses and took a seat where the guards directed them to, each being given their own private seat, to avoid territorial disputes. Abraham followed the other inmates onto the bus and was seated around the middle. When he was settled, he closed his eyes and laid his head against the back of his seat. It was comfortable enough and he was expecting it to be a long, cold bus ride. He didn't want make the mistake of accidently provoking an attack from one of the other inmates by innocently looking around either, so he attempted to put his nerves to rest. He slowly drifted away to sleep, through the foreign bodily sounds coming from the other inmates all around him.

Abraham woke with alarm, lurching forward, as the bus came to a sudden stop. One of the guards rushed through the walkway of the bus as Abraham turned to look at the disturbance near the back. One of the younger men was gasping for air, being strangled by a more weathered looking man in the seat behind him. The man had only a few rotted teeth in his mouth, but he was giving off a smile that shinned more brightly than any smile Abraham had ever seen. Abraham had never felt the gratification of achieving a vice so long lusted after as this man was feeling. It even stirred a longing in Abraham, to feel something even close to this, as horrific as it was. Anything to be as happy as that man was at the moment. As the man being strangled gasped for air with his wide eye's bulging out of their sockets, everyone on the bus watched, this being the best entertainment most of them had seen in a while. It was short lived, because the guard who had rushed past grabbed his club and began hitting the strangler relentlessly. When the man had lost a good bit of blood and was nearing unconsciousness, the guard released him from his chains and pulled him from his seat, dragged him through the walkway like a rag doll, and threw him off the front entrance of the bus. The man hit the snowy ground hard and rolled a couple feet, his blood staining the snow where he went. The man then raised his bloodied face to watch as the guard calmly stepped off the bus and walked menacingly toward him. Abraham stared from the window expecting an execution. The guard kicked the inmate's raised, pleading head; blood and teeth went flying out of his mouth. The guard then coolly took out his pistol from its holster and shot the man twice in each leg; one in the thigh and one in the shin. He turned to re-enter the bus, leaving his victim half dead and screaming through his bloodied mouth in the blizzard.[mention the blizzard earlier in the paragraph]

Normally, Abraham would have thought that the guard was trying to set an example for the other inmates, but under the circumstances he suspected that the guard was only being cruel for his own amusement. As the bus started to move again, Abraham saw the man outside begging for the bus to come back and save him, hoping for any other fate. Abraham closed his eyes hoping to rid the atrocious scene from his memory with sleep, but even in his dreams the man's bloody screaming was as vivid as it was in life.

When they'd arrived at an old, fenced in, prison camp, they were herded around as the superior officers tried to mold them into something usable. Abraham and the other prisoners did as they were told, some trying harder than others and completely buying into the ideology that was drilled into them daily, but all were glad to have something to fill up their time. There were a few more encounters like the one on the bus but nothing unexpected, or nearly as brutal. They were prisoners being released after all serving years in solitary confinement, so it was expected that there would be disputes as they readjusted to life.

During shooting practice Abraham found that he wasn't bad with a rifle. Maybe he should have been a soldier all along. He concentrated on his aim and pulled back the cold metal trigger hitting the plastic dummy with the bullet almost consistently. He noticed that further down on the poorly constructed shooting range he had someone watching him. The man tried to act inconspicuous but Abraham saw through it. He looked about the age Abraham guessed that he himself was, but the man was in worse shape.

Just like Abraham had thought it would be, most of the food was sent to the soldiers in the field and the left over scrapes were given to the scum within the camp. It was lucky to find a mouse, or some other small rodent or bug that could have only of gotten to the snowy isolated base, by riding in one of the trucks that came bearing supplies. The nights were typically hard to get to sleep as well. Abraham was uneasy about sleeping out in the open with the other inmates, especially the one who had been watching him. The handcuffs restraining his arms didn't help him feel any better, but at the same time it was less unnerving knowing that the rest of the inmates were handcuffed as well. He tried closing his eyes and calming himself down. He'd been here almost 2 and a-half weeks now, but it was still hard for him to get anywhere near comfortable enough so that he could fall asleep. He took a deep breath and tried thinking of memories from his childhood. It helped him to try and think of calming memories from his past, as few as there were. Childhood innocence is too pure to corrupt which is the reason he found such solace in them. Being too old for childhood ignorance and too young to be old and wise, puts man in a complicated spot of trying to constantly understand himself, and his surroundings. Being a child had freed him from that unsettling feeling that haunted Abraham in his adulthood, the feeling of being constantly worried over meaningless things, and that's what Abraham was looking for in his memories. It worked but only just. The slightest cough or loud snore could have taken him away, back to the present. But tonight it was the soft scurry of footsteps.

They were careful, calculated steps and were getting closer for every steadily increasing breath Abraham took. He felt his entire body strain in agitation. He was like a lamb for the slaughter. He tried getting free of his restraints but it was useless. He was helpless and he was going to die. The man walked up beside Abraham's cot and didn't take his gaze off of him "What do you want?" Abraham demanded furiously, his heart almost choking him from its thunderous beating. He glared perversely at the man, waiting for either an answer or his death. It was the man who had been watching him at the range. He had short dark hair and had a defined, yet physical looking face, a couple of scars cut across the side of it from whatever or whoever had been trying to kill him.

"Don't worry I'm not going to kill you. Handy skill being able to pick locks," he whispered with a grin, trying to make a joke of it. He had a couple of metal fillings over his teeth, of which he seemed to have most of. Abraham hadn't even thought of how the man had gotten out of his bed in the suspense. Abraham didn't say anything; he just continued staring defiantly at the man. If this was to be his end then he was going to give the man as little satisfaction as possible. The man leaned closer to Abraham, so much so that Abraham could feel the man's hot, stinking breath on his face. "I want to ask you something," the man whispered sincerely, jerking his head psychotically behind him as if he expected someone to be there and then calmly returned his gaze to Abraham.

"One of these days they'll ship us out to the war and you bet your ass we'll all die."

Now Abraham understood.

"I can get us away from the battle and the soldiers, but I won't be able to do it alone. My gut feeling tells me I can trust you, so until the time comes think about it. Oh, and my names Ivan," he hastily murmured and then the man named Ivan slowly turned around and went back to his cot.

Abraham heard the click of what must have been his handcuffs relocking. His body began to calm down but, only to give way to his unease about what the man had said. He wanted to escape. To freedom, something Abraham had not even believed could be a realistic dream for him again but the mere suggestion of it was intoxicating. The idea was simple enough, but when it came down to it something would prevent it from becoming a reality for Abraham. It'd be best to not even give in to the thought, because doing so would make him no better than any of the other fools here who had submitted to the idea of a future. A few minutes later the watch guard came back from the bathroom.

Chapter 3

The weeks of training passed and the men were finally sent out on several large trucks after so much anxious waiting. In what little briefing they had been given, the prisoners were told that they were on route to retake the port city of Yakutsk. Nothing further had been revealed; not who they were fighting, or even why. Captains had been assigned to groups of 30 or so, and it was to them that the details resided in. It didn't matter though; the prisoners would do what they were told regardless of being kept in the dark.

As the convoy of soldiers drove through the eastern wilderness of Russia, the snow began letting up week by week. The occasional snow storm would still come and go, but it never lasted as long as it did the time before. Sometimes after a light snowfall came, the dirt roads became too muddy to drive the large trucks through, and the convoy would stop for a couple of days till it was dry or refrozen enough to drive through. Those occurrences were often peaceful, sleeping in a tent and watching the sun set and rise over the snowy forests. It was almost as if there was nothing else but the wilderness. No trace of the atrociousness of humanity. The pleasant weather setting the mood, as various animals trampled through the trees and the wet green plains on the sides of the road. It had been a long, quiet couple of weeks, and Abraham would miss them when they arrived at the destination.

Some of the inmates had had the same idea as Ivan, but were premature about it and were shot almost as instantly as they ran. Abraham had just spent every waking moment thinking of what he might do, or what it would be like when he escaped. How would he feel about freedom? He knew that it was unlikely that they would get away but the thought of it was intoxicating. He had given in to the hope of survival like many of the other men, though his reason was different, he still felt like a fool. He had no family to go see, nor any longing for indulgences. Was surviving to see the world again even something he wanted to do? What would he do with freedom? After so long of rotting in a cell he had nothing left he wanted from the outside world. He was terrified of the thought of freedom.

The trucks engine made a loud, exasperating noise as if it was about to blow. They must have gotten stuck in the mud again. The flap near the back of the truck opened, and a commanding officer was in the opening.

"Everyone get out! We're close enough that we'll just walk from here on to the city."

The men started getting up and grabbing their gear. Abraham got to his feet and swung his rifle strap around his shoulder and waited in line to get off the back of the truck. He jumped out, and as he landed he realized just how muddy it was. Water and mud went clear up to his boots laces. A disgusted look came over his face as he thought of the long road ahead. He trudged over to the flooded grassy sides of the road on the outskirts of the forest, where it would be easier to walk, and waited with the other men. He looked around and over a long way off in the twilight he could make out large snowy mountains beyond the forests and rivers. Mountains that were towering out from the earth, looking more majestic than life could in its best of forms. Always at the center of romanticism in the human mind, yet the true symbolism is something more clandestine. That something, however hard Abraham tried to look for it, always remained a mystery to him though, as well as most other men, but he was still captivated by them.

An order must have been given from somewhere ahead, because everyone started moving forward, splashing water, mud, and grass up as they walked. Hours passed and signs of exhaustion were obvious in the men; the sweating, staggering, and occasional tripping, but at least from what Abraham knew, they weren't stopping anytime soon. Wiping the sweat from his brow, he scanned the crowd of soldiers in front and behind of him and to his sides but couldn't see Ivan anywhere. He was starting to wonder if the man had been disingenuous, or had chosen someone else, or even if he had decided against it after all from watching the other failed attempts.

The night had almost cast the earth in shadow for the night and Abraham was beginning to be able to make out the distant lights of a city far ahead. It seemed like a pretty well sized city as far as he could tell. Having never been to the east, he wondered if the towns would look the same, or if they would be different from the modern cities he had been too in the west. Before Abraham had perceived what was going on, he heard the sounds of loud machine gun shots and explosions from somewhere in front of him. Screaming and mass confusion broke out everywhere. Men were scattering and falling down all around, but amidst the chaos he herd an order yelled out to go into the woods for cover, and everyone around started frantically running toward the forest.

Abraham kept low and ran in, taking cover behind a tree with a great big trunk. Another man came over to the same tree and fell down quickly with his back against the tree. His eyes were closed in fright and it even looked like he was praying. He was a young man who didn't look as though he belonged in battle, let alone at the prison. There wasn't enough room behind the tree to hide both of them, so they struggled between one another, both trying to get more cover than what they had. Mud and dirt started flying up around the tree. More frantically now the two of them struggled between each other for more cover. Suddenly the pressure against him stopped and a hot liquid sprayed across Abrahams face and blinded him for a second before wiping it away from his eyes. He turned his head quickly to see that the young man beside him had been shot; a hole had indented his skull from beside his left ear and exited through his left eye socket. There was bloody bone and brain all over Abraham's clothes, as well the young man's face and body. Abraham pushed the lifeless body out of the way so he could take full cover and then he closed his eyes trying to calm himself down and prevent his stomach from vomiting. What a waste. A young man had lost his life for nothing. Even if he had done something wrong he hadn't deserved this. Abraham reopened his eyes and turned his head to look at the young man once more. There were tear stains through the dirt on his cheeks that had collected after weeks of not washing. In the moonlight Abraham saw his reflection in the pool of blood collecting around the young man's head, as he lay motionless on the soggy ground. He wiped the sweat from his brow, heavily breathing in and out, turning to look the other way feeling sick to his stomach and shaking uncontrollably. He saw another tree that would give him good cover up ahead; anything to get away from the young man's body.

As he prepared to run over to it, the thought of just trying to get himself killed crossed his mind. It's what he had signed up for in the first place and had only gotten sidetracked by the lure of freedom. So why shouldn't he take the opportunity and end things here and now instead of procrastinating it out? Life was cruel, and from what he remembered it wasn't much better even when he was a free man all that time ago. But he couldn't know for sure that things wouldn't be different. The endless dreaming the last few weeks had instilled just enough curiosity and hope that even the thought of being able to avoid more traumatic memories couldn't displace.

He started running for the tree. He ran as fast as he could but it still seemed as though he was running for hours. Only 5 more yards left. Mid-stride, he felt a strong force pulling him backward and down to the ground. His legs flew up in the air and Abraham hit the soft ground hard, the wind leaving his lungs, but his adrenaline held him and he quickly turned on his stomach to see what had pulled him down. He was surprised to see that it was the man named Ivan. He was staring at Abraham motioning to him to stay down. Abraham nodded and slowly crawled closer to him to see what he had planned. "There's two coming on the right. You take the furthest one." Ivan whispered breathlessly. Abraham looked to where he was pointing and vaguely saw the shadowy figures moving through the brush. He brought his rifle up so the barrel was propped up by his left arm lying on the ground in front of him. He took aim. His arm was shaking so uncontrollably that he was afraid to take the shot for fear of missing. Ivan must have been waiting on him to shoot first, from his hesitation. Abraham breathed in and out slowly though his nose, doing everything he could to calm himself. His trigger finger was trembling, anxiously waiting for Abraham to decide to shoot. The shadowy figure stopped moving and was looking at something on the ground. Now was the time. Abraham breathed in and slowly exhaled. Finally his finger got its chance and clamped down hard on the trigger. The gun went off with a loud burst as the gun powder ignited, and then almost in unison Ivan's went off. Ivan was grinning happily about the feat, as the shadows fell.

"Follow me now," he whispered unable to contain his excitement, and stood up off the ground. Abraham got to his feet after Ivan and began running after him crouched down through the brush, dodging tree limbs and bushes as they went.

The fighting was still going on, but was getting more and more distant as they ran through the dark forest. As malnourished as they were from the past weeks, they ran for hours purely on the adrenaline of the night. After some time Ivan finally stopped in a small clearing, and the two of them fell down exhausted from the run. After catching taking a moment to catch his breath Ivan said in broken sentences, "let's sleep here for a couple of hours and then get going again." He dug into one of his shirts pouches and brought out what looked like a piece of paper and something else that Abraham couldn't see as well under the moonlight. Abraham heard a grinding noise and then Ivan's face lit up, uncovering the identity of the items he held. One was a silver rectangular cigarette lighter and the other was a map from one of the officers.

"Alright, from what I can tell we were headed northeast to Yakutsk and we ran into that fight about four miles out. My best guess is that we go to Magan which is about nine miles away from Yakutsk. Judging from how long we ran I'd say we have about another couple hours left till we reach the outskirts of the city."

"What do we do once we get to the city?" Abraham asked exhausted.

"We'll get a hotel I guess to rest for the day. Then I'm going to take a train to Yekaterinburg where my brother lives... You can come if you'd like. I could even get you a job," Ivan asked trying to be careful so that he didn't overstep.

Abraham thought about this. "What kind of a job?"

Ivan smiled laying his head back for sleep. "I'll tell you about it tomorrow."

Abraham nodded, still heavily breathing, and laid back feeling uneasy, though he didn't have much of a choice but to trust the man. He closed his eyes and tried to sleep even though he knew it would take a while. He listened to the sounds of the forest, the wind gently blowing the trees back and forth, and a long way off he could still make out the sounds of the battle. It was almost peaceful and the ground made for a softer bed than he'd had in years. He couldn't stop running things through his mind. The events of the night plagued him, and thoughts of the future were unsettling as well. He had been cut off from any type of social contact with people for the longest time, so perhaps his suspicions of Ivan were just the social anxiety that he was feeling. Enough time passed and regardless of the night, blissful unconsciousness came to Abraham, without even a dream to poison his mind.

Chapter 4

After waking up early as the sun crossed the boundary into the sky, the two men walked through a vastly wooded forest for several miles, now calmer that they were no longer fleeing. Eventually the forest let out to engulfing gray planes expanding over the hills, probably used for farmland after the colder seasons had passed, and a little ways off in the distance they could make out the blurry outlines making up the city of Magan.

It was an old little town, with a lake at the heart of it, giving it life. Full of herdsmen, farmers, fishermen and occasionally the small business man, it was a simple town that had never really seen much and perhaps that's what drew Abraham to it. Time had passed, but the city had never paid much attention to it and went about its own business, unconcerned with the troubles of the modern world. The rural look of all the buildings and people gave him comfort, as though their simplicity would keep him from the reality of his situation or even his past. It was welcoming enough, he felt as though he could stay here and start an entirely new life. No further worries about his purpose or fate, only simplistic living until a peaceful breeze came for him like a whisper. His previous life would entirely fade from memory and would hold no further grasp over him. But it was foolish to think that. Eventually his past would catch up with him and he would only be ripped away from another life as he had already been. His heart wanted truth and even though the town could give him the serenity he longed for, he would never truly feel as though he belonged there. He'd seen too much and the town had seen too little for them to ever coincide together.

Abraham followed Ivan through the city watching the townspeople go about their business, walking in and out of old buildings, built of brick and an oddly painted wood, and they walked along the cracking stone sidewalk until they came to a tall, reddish building with numerous windows and duel black entry doors. "I think this must be it," Ivan said questionably. Abraham looked up and saw the sign that hung above the doors. "Magan's Finest" it read in black letters against a chipping white background.

Ivan opened the door and proceeded in, followed closely by Abraham. They walked towards a desk at which a balding middle aged man sat behind. He was reading a newspaper through thin spectacles and lazily smoking on a half smoked cigarette, explaining the smoky musk that met them as they entered.

"Can I help you boys?" the man behind the desk asked without glancing away from his paper.

"...uh yeah. Can we get a room? This is a motel right?"

"Yes," the man behind the desk said annoyed at the question and probably more so that he had to redirect his attention away from the paper. "It's thirty rubles per night.

We only take hard currency, so you know, in case your one of those westerners that only has electronic cash."

"No that's fine; we'll take a room then," Ivan said pulling out a wallet to Abraham's surprise. It must have been the officer's that Ivan had somehow robbed blind. Or looted, either way it was doing the two of them a hell of a lot more good, than it would have the officer.

Ivan paid the man and was given a small copper key. It must have had the room number on it because without further direction Ivan backed away looking questionably at the man behind the desk who had started reading again. The attendant wasn't much for hospitality apparently. Ivan finally turned around and jerked his neck beckoning Abraham to follow him. They took a left down the hallway beside the desk. The doors to the rooms were old and red, with a rusty golden handle. It had probably been a nice motel when it was first made, judging by the red carpet and various decorations along the wall, but time had taken its toll on it and it no longer was what it had been once. They stopped short of the last few doors and opened the door to their right, the handle creaking loudly as if it hadn't been turned in years. Abraham followed Ivan in and saw the poorly furnished room. There was a single bed with a burgundy comforter covered in dust and a toilet with black water to their left as soon as they entered; only separated by a thin short wall. Spider webs covered the peeling, once cream colored walls in lucrative designs, looking almost as if it had been on purpose to add to the overall feeling of the room. No window, only a dim overhead light that occasionally flickered. Ivan must have seen Abraham analyzing the room.

"It's better than your cell is it not?" Ivan laughed.

"Yeah, it's just been awhile since I've seen an actual room."

"Well you'll have it basically all day to yourself. I'm going to go find some money to get us train tickets. Hopefully they have a phone or something at the desk so I can call my brother. I'll be back in a while."

With that he nodded at Abraham and left the room shutting the door quietly behind him. Abraham kept staring at the decomposing room. It wasn't the vulgarity that caught his attention, the prison had been insurmountably worse. What had caught his eye and was the cause of his discomfort, was a little dark wooden clock on the nightstand beside the bed. He'd owned the same clock for some time before he went to prison. It had been both of theirs, a wedding present from an acquaintance that Abraham no longer remembered in any detail. He'd never liked the ugly little thing, but she'd just put it in the kitchen. She was like that as far back as Abraham could remember, never wanting to upset anyone even on such small a thing as gifts. What had gone so wrong for things to end as they had? Had they slowly grown apart from one another, too worried over money, or other things of no conscious? Abraham had loved her and she had felt the same way too at one point. He would have done anything for her, but he was blind to what was happening and everything he did to bring her back only pushed her farther away. It was all his fault. She'd deserved better than him but he'd been too convincing to the point of even fooling himself that he was ready.

The stresses of life escalated through the years and at the climax of his indiscretion and clouded judgment, he found himself sitting outside of his house with a small six shooter pistol he'd bought and had been holding onto, hoping that she would come back to him so he wouldn't need it. The hopelessness of his situation gave him just enough courage to do what he thought he had no other choice in. She thought he was at work. He should have been at work, not here. Not about to do what he was dead set on doing. To him the choice was simple. Either let your life crash around you as the only thing you ever loved leaves you. Or end everything and ultimately he saw no other way out. He could not live without her in his life. He opened the door to his old black truck, and not even bothering to shut it ran up to his house, the height of the moment fueling his adrenaline. He shoved open the door and ran through the hallway back to the bedroom. Even as he'd entered he heard them. The door was locked as he fumbled with the door knob still trying to open it in his madness. She was half screaming, half crying trying to say something to calm him down. Abraham jerked his leg up and smashed it into the door, slamming the broken thing against the wall as it opened. He'd never felt worse; helpless and angry. Hurt mostly. He felt the tears starting to come to his eyes. He paid them no attention even as they blurred his vision. He raised the pistol to the man's direction and squeezed the trigger. The sound and aftermath were a lot different from what Abraham had been expecting. Blood was all over the poorly painted walls that he'd painted himself a couple years ago. Her blood curdling screams barely fazed him as he looked in terror at what he'd done. He pointed the gun mechanically at her as she cowered in the corner of the room holding up her hands as if to stop what was happening. He looked at her beautiful crying face that he used to love so much, feeling as though the world was collapsing. How could she have done this to him? How could he have done this to her? There was no turning back now though. He closed his eyes and squeezed the trigger and after one last high pitched frightened scream, there was silence in the room, but that last scream echoed throughout Abraham's entire being.

He stood there with his eyes closed, too cowardly to see the aftermath of his insanity. He slowly opened his eyes to see the blood covered room. Bits of flesh and bone and wood from the door he'd kicked in covered the floor. The sick feeling he'd had all week had reached its breaking point and after dropping the gun, he dropped to his knees uncontrollably convulsing. As he puked he only felt worse than before. He had to get out of this room. He got up off his knees, turning around and stumbled through the broken doorway trying not to think. What had he done? He'd expected to feel something better since having done this, some sort of resolution, but he only felt a hollow pain, as if nothing would ever again comfort him. He stumbled drunkenly into the living room and fell down on the couch. He couldn't stop going over every little memory they had had. The good and the bad, he missed them both. Wished he could change everything. Wish she had never met him. Wish that he had never been born or had died as a child from some disease, as his baby sister had. Wish something different. Suicide had been his original intent for his own personal resolution but the realization of the situation put him into shock, paralyzing him. Why, was the only question he had, but to that he would never get an answer, and in his heart he knew this.

That's where the police had found him. So much time had passed since then, yet it seemed as though no time at all had. Wiping away the tears he walked over to the bed and sat down. He had been a stupid and blind man then. He was someone else now or at least he hoped he was. The prison had, as well as changing him for the worse, had given him time to think about everything, giving him the wisdom that he hoped had changed him. With all the time in the world to think you tend to become a bit thoughtless and now with this resurgence of memories he couldn't help run it through his mind back and forth, disgusted with the coward he used to be, but unable to change the past. However much he wishes he could have stopped himself, he knew there was nothing he could do now. It was over. He lay down and slowly drifted away but all the while he didn't stop thinking about her.

Chapter 5

Abraham awoke as he heard the door gently open and close.

"Sorry I didn't mean to wake you," Ivan said apologetically as he walked slowly into the old room. "I got us the tickets to Yekaterinburg, where my brother lives... And a bit of food," he added, as he handed a small paper bag with dark crusted bread and oily white cheese to Abraham. "My brother will meet us at the train station when we get there. If that's what you're still planning on doing?" he questioned.

"I am. I have nothing else waiting for me," Abraham said, sounding unintentionally gloomy, as he started eating the bread and cheese. A concerned look came over Ivan's face but he was quick to change the subject.

"So what were you in that prison for anyways?" he asked curiously.

Abraham paused once again recalling the memory. "I don't really want to talk about it," he said reserved, hoping that Ivan would accept his answer.

"That's fine," Ivan said raising his eyebrows and nodding. "Plenty of guys that go in don't like talking about it. I've been in too often to care what people think." He laughed.

Abraham smiled back as he took bites of cheese and bread.

"Yeah I got brought in after me and a couple guys went and tried to rob some heroin dealers. Turned out to be a bust though...big fucking mess," he finished, hoping to have rendered some sort of response from Abraham.

Abraham just awkwardly looked at the floor though. He knew Ivan could sense how uneasy he felt about being in the world again but neither man said anything. Abraham was glad about that. "We leave tonight at 9 so get some more rest, I'll be back. I'm going to go get us a little more money," Ivan said as he headed toward the door, having finally gotten the hint that Abraham wanted to be alone. Abraham got up off the bed and put the cheese and bread he hadn't finished on the nightstand beside the clock. He lay back down on the dusty mattress and tried to sleep, but just ended up resting his eyes. He laid there and thought more, hoping to resolve his anxiety with some sort of internal revelation but nothing came.

Ivan returned a couple hours later with more food and some clothes. Abraham sat up on the bed curiously.

"What are the clothes for?"

"We can't be walking around in military outfits." Ivan laughed. "I'm surprised no one's said anything yet but they probably have scouts coming through the town all the time. Let's get dressed and then well head to the station."

Ivan handed the folded rustic clothes to Abraham and they both started getting dressed. As Abraham was tying up his boots he decided that now was as good a time as any to ask Ivan about the job.

"What's the job your brother has for us?"

Ivan looked stunned for a second and then relaxed his face. "I guess you should know what you'll be getting into," he said regrettably. "How much do you know about genetics?"

"Not much. They were advertising for them before I went away."

"You were away for a while then," Ivan said surprised, looking up at Abraham as he buttoned his shirt. "Everyone pretty much now has them, or at least the people with the money to buy them." He finished lacing up his boots and stood, leaning against the wall. "Well my brother runs a company, kind of, but anyways he sells genetics that he produces. It's not quite legal though because he doesn't have a license and he sells them way below hospital prices. All we'll be doing is providing some assistance to him. He's not really much for muscle so he may need protection sometimes or he might just need us to go collect a debt occasionally; nothing big."

Abraham nodded thinking deeply about what Ivan had said. Genetics; it was an old controversial memory. Everyone was excited about it, but still, some worried about the side effects of tampering with human DNA. Abraham was too young and too poor to care about what was going on in the upper class of society back then. He'd already survived through the end of the eugenics craze, though he himself had been sterilized in accordance with his prison sentence, but after a while human engineering had just lost its interest. He had had more important things on his mind. Genetics seemed to have just become another product for consumers like candy bars, not particularly something people needed. Abraham recalled watching the CEO of one of the genetics companies giving a speech on television. The man was middle aged and seemed very enthusiastic about what he was saying. "...The world started eugenics as a way to save and improve humanity, making it as unflawed as possible in conjunction with human nature. Since it was started, and then perfected by our furors in Germany, it has improved the human way of life and now we're as strong a race as there's ever been... And now finally, thanks to UCB Industries, we have the opportunity to make our race even better. This isn't just enhancing your-self as a person. This is man-made evolution..." It would be interesting to see how genetics had turned out for society. Or better yet, what they had turned society into. He hoped things might be like the world he'd left but truthfully he knew better than that. It'd been a long time and genetics were different than eugenics. Eugenics took time to completely wipe out genes through sterilization and then condense all the "good" genes into a family which then took generations. Genetics could be done in a matter of week's maybe less. He was probably going back to a world that he no longer knew and that no longer knew him.

"You ready?" Ivan said.

Abraham looked at the clock, anxious from the thought. It read 8:34 p.m.

"Sure." He got up off the bed and leaving the first room he'd stayed in for years, followed Ivan out the door.

Chapter 6

The train station looked much like the rest of the town; old red brick with cement floors and antique looking benches. It had all been left behind through the passing of time and compared to the electrical trains that flew in and out of the train station at speeds that Abraham found hard to believe, it was as if the two eras of civilization were colliding. They were metallic, thin little trains and to the eye didn't seem that they would be all that spacious on the inside.

There was only two other people that appeared to be waiting on the same train as they were. An old man with a long white beard and a little girl, most likely his granddaughter. She was cute, not more than 8, with little red strap on slippers and a long plaid skirt. Her facial expression looked like most children do when they are being directed somewhere and they don't fully understand what's going on. Blank and trying to take in everything, maybe a little scared. She'd probably come to stay with her grandfather for the winter or spring season and was now returning home to the city for school.

"Here come's our train," said Ivan pointing to where he saw the train coming into the station. Abraham looked to where Ivan had directed and saw the machine as it slowed down, coming to a halt in front of them, screeching as it did so. When the door to the train opened only a hand full of people got off the train, many of which looking like the general townspeople had. Ivan followed the old man and little girl onto the train and Abraham in turn followed him. The inside was nice enough but a little worn from use. Abraham followed Ivan back to a corridor near the back of the train car. Once Ivan reached one he liked enough, he stopped and opened the compartment hoping that no one was inside. No one was. It was a small, plain compartment with two gray cushioned benches facing each other and a window to the outside against the far wall.

They walked in and took seats nearest the window. As they waited for the train to start moving Abraham looked out the window and watched as more people began to come and go through the train station now that the day was picking up. Someone knocked at the compartments door. "Hello?" a woman's voice asked. Ivan cautiously stood up and went to open the door. It was a beautiful young blonde girl.

"Can we help you?" Ivan asked politely. Anyone else would have thought the suddenness in his voice was from the attractive woman but Abraham knew better being what their situation was.

"Hi, welcome aboard can I get you anything, a paper, some coffee?" she asked politely and smiling. "We'll take a paper," Ivan said relaxing and pulling out a couple of rubbles. She handed him the paper in exchange for the rubles and left. Ivan closed the compartment door and went back to sitting down, reading the paper as he did so. "Look at the glorious victory we've won," Ivan said over exaggerating "glorious" and handing the paper to Abraham, smirking. Abraham took it and read the headline on the front page. *"Port City of Yakutsk Taken from Rebels by Sea Invasion"*

So the prisoners were a decoy so the real army could take the city without as much resistance. It wasn't surprising. Abraham couldn't help but think of the boy that'd been shot beside him during the battle. Sent to his death for nothing. Waste of life. The prisoners weren't even mentioned, though if it was released to the public, there probably would have been outrage against rapists and murders being let out of prison and being given weapons.

He folded the newspaper up at the creases and handed it back to Ivan who threw it on the seat beside himself. Ivan then pulled out a pack of cigarettes and took one out. He set the pack down beside him and pulled out the lighter he'd gotten the night of the escape and struck a light.

Abraham looked out the window to see the older man from earlier waving goodbye to the little girl who must have been in a compartment toward the middle. The train's overhead speaker came on and the conductor began speaking about the trip. Once he stopped talking, the train began slowly moving and the old man waving good-bye at his granddaughter grew farther, and farther away as the train gained speed, ending the little girl's stay as the season changed. Abraham kept looking out the window even as the country landscape that they had begun to travel through became a blur of flashing browns and greens and blues.

Away from humanity, the earth always has a transcendental beauty about it. This was true before he went to prison and remained so. Unfaltering even in the most horrific of times, it brought Abraham to a feeling that he'd not felt in quite a while. Calm, without the sense of urgency he'd felt ever since being released from prison. The earth was the earth, despite of what was happening and it would remain so even when it was all done. But now that the train had reached its full traveling speed he no longer was able to enjoy it. Ivan had begun reading the paper again and now there was nothing for Abraham to do but try and get some more sleep. He lay down as best he could in the small compartment and closed his eyes. As sometimes things are, getting to sleep was difficult. He was too anxious about reaching the city and what would happen there. Things would be different but how different? Could he adapt or was he doomed to fail? Abraham tossed questions around in his head for a while but in time his mind slowed and he drifted away.

When he awoke he was no longer on the train but sitting on a small dirt covered mound in the middle of a morning lake, with the dew floating above the water, adding a misty look to it. There was a few weeds growing on the mound but for the most part the dirt was very poor and dark. It was pitch black out save for the moon and it was shining at its fullest revealing every discolorment on it. He began hearing someone calling him. It was like a whisper in the wind at first but became clearer. It was a woman's voice but it was too far off to be distinguishable. He shakily stood up and turned around, trying to find where the noise was coming from. He walked to the edge of the mound, his feet sinking in the soft dirt, and saw something shimmering in the water near the bank of the mound.

He kneeled down and submerged his arm underwater grabbing at the shimmering item. The water was warm and thick. When he pulled his arm from the water it was covered in dark red blood. It wasn't water that surrounded him he realized, falling back in surprise. Startled as he was, he saw the item that had caught his eye. It was a small golden locket. He slowly opened it, his heart beating faster and faster as he began to recognize the object. Inside was a picture of him and his wife but all the features of their faces were missing. He dropped the locket and started crawling backward but lost his balance and fell down into the lake. His head became submerged beneath the blood and he felt as though he was sinking endlessly.

Grasping for air but nothing came except the warm, salty liquid, slowly filling his lunges. He woke with a start and saw that Ivan was standing over him and had been trying to wake him. Ivan gave him a curious look. "We've arrived."

Chapter 7

As Abraham stepped off the train he instantly felt a nervous impulse to get back on. It was as if they had taken a time machine, the lights, clothing, even the floors were alien to anything Abraham had seen before. It was horrifying. It was incredible. The walls had become a mural of holograms advertising this and that; beautiful men and women, telling him what he needed to become happier and more complete; some advertising food, others clothing, and so on with the same approach. There were so many lights in such an enclosed area. There probably had even been a lot of lights and holograms when they went underground while he was sleeping on the train. Abraham looked up and saw that the ceilings of the underground train station even had advertising flying across them, as if the ceiling was one giant television screen. There were so many colors. Bright reds and blues and yellows all so vivid that one felt as though the images were there to comfort, instead of convince you of the longing to fill the emptiness inside of yourself.

Ivan stopped a few feet ahead of Abraham and looked behind him, seeing that Abraham had backed back up onto the train. It must have been in his face. "You okay? Just wait until you see the city. Come on."

His trance being broken, Abraham adolescently hurried up to Ivan and tried to stay close so he didn't drown in the ocean of people. Some of them were dressed in sleek, black suits that Abraham had never seen, some dressed in variants of the clothes he'd grown up seeing, and others dressed in worse clothes than he and Ivan had on. Particularly the lonesome, sad people, curled up in corners like a stain on the pearly white floor. It was a bit cold down there but Abraham's senses were still numb from the prison. He figured it would take a while for them to come back as strong as they were, that is if they even did come back.

They walked through the station bumping into people as frequently as they seemed to get bumped into themselves. Abraham couldn't believe how different things looked. It's true that he'd never been to this city before, but everyone he'd ever been to didn't look anything like this. It was beautiful but terrifying, and everywhere people walked about paying no attention, consumed with their lives. Abraham didn't have eyes big enough to take in everything he wanted to. He did his best to keep following Ivan through the crowd feeling boyish, like it was the first time he'd ever been to the circus. They kept walking, every now and then taking an escalator up to a higher platform. The station was enormous and went deep into the earth, making it quite a long walk from where they had begun. It was mapped out over several miles, every platform having a slight escalation leading up toward the surface where Ivan and Abraham were headed, with various shops taking advantage of the large layout. Always white marble floors, with all the walls and furniture being a shiny metallic black, probably so that the holograms showed up better, but it made for a seemingly bleak environment. After a while, the advertisements lost their appeal and made the entire place feel a little more anxious. At first it was just amazing because of the vividness but now they added tension and made it feel as though they were being bombarded by all sides. It became more overwhelming the longer they stayed in the station.

"There he is," Ivan said excitedly, not bothering to look back at Abraham, but even so Abraham knew he was smiling. The man Ivan was talking about was an older, brownish-gray haired man, probably in his late 40's, early 50's, sitting on a bench by one of the walls. The black suit he was wearing was like many of the other expensive looking attire that Abraham had seen around the station. The lines in his face held time in them and were scrunched up, making a concentrated frown upon his brow. He might have seen them coming if his attention hadn't been focused on a device he had sitting on the little stand in front of his chair.

As they walked closer, Abraham saw it was projecting something into the air that the man was interacting with, but Abraham didn't have enough time to see exactly what it was.

"Michael!" Ivan yelled happily.

The man looked up surprised but his expression instantly changed into a smile.

"Ivan?" He stood up and the men hurried to embrace each other.

"It's been too long." Ivan said.

"It's good to see you," Michael exclaimed overjoyed.

"This is the man I told you about over the phone. Abraham, this is my brother Michael." Ivan said gesturing the introduction with his hand and Abraham reached out to shake Michael's.

"It's good to meet you finally. Ivan said you needed a job as well?"

"You too and yeah that's right if you have anything."

"Good there's always something to do and if you need anything else just ask. You did a lot to help Ivan, I only want to return the favor." He laughed happily looking back at Ivan. "Let's get out of this place then, all these holograms are starting to bother me; didn't use to be as clustered as this," Michael said disgustedly looking around.

The men started walking and Abraham noticed a couple of stocky men were following them, Michael's bodyguards from the way he seemed to order them around.

"I've set you both up with an apartment, so you won't have to go to the store or anything for a while."

"That's good; we'll probably just stay in tonight anyways," Ivan said.

"Sounds good, but tomorrow were going out to celebrate the return of my brother," Michael said kissing his brother happily on the cheek. Ivan smiled.

"Anything you say," Ivan said happily.

As they walked, Michael and Ivan kept talking, but Abraham's attention was more focused on the large opening half a mile ahead of them. They kept ascending the escalating floor and the further they went, the more lights Abraham started to be able to make out in the opening. At first it was just a blur of neon and fluorescent lights but as they drew further toward the mouth he started to be able to make out all the glowing signs hanging on skyscraping buildings; Holograms projecting into the air so real that it looked as if there was a beautiful giant smiling down upon the city, holding an electric blue bottle. It was heart stopping. Abraham couldn't believe anything like this existed or even could exist. Highways were suspended in the air, with bright streams of light flying over them as they twisted around the great skyscrapers of the city. The architecture of the buildings was just as magnificent as the actual height of the buildings. One in particular had a wide base followed by a slender body and then a circular top, only beautified more by the looping suspended highways, almost making a circle around the top as if making a frame for the spectacle. Many others had a thin oval architecture, the rectangular prism architecture of the past being a rarity. Even though it was night the city was lit up as if it was just a cloudy day. Everything had a bright fluorescent light on it, intensifying the feeling of magnificence that emanated from the city.

Abraham tripped a little as he went outside barely noticing that they had made it out of the station. "You okay?" Michael asked, him and Ivan both laughing. Abraham smiled back at them embarrassed. There were so many people in the stone courtyard where the station had come up at; sitting in benches, dancing, and talking, all around a great fountain in the center. Across the street from the courtyard, Abraham saw people outside on a patio suspended off the third level of the building, yelling and laughing happily. All were dressed in sleek suits and beautiful dresses. Some of the dresses had vivid flowers blossoming and other designs wavering and changing color on them. There were people all over the street as well, walking here and there, some stumbling from one place to the next, Others just walking along euphorically as if they were actually somewhere else.

"The car's over here." Michael directed them. Abraham now saw the tremendous concave of the station extending some six stories in the air in a slow ovate shape. He followed Michael and Ivan around the side of the station over to a large circle drive with another large fountain at the center, which was used as a pickup from the station. Michael walked over to an elongated, shiny, white car. It had metallic silver rims, almost completely covered by the cars exterior and thick black tires so dark that it was a question if they were even made out of rubber.

As they came close the back doors opened to the sky as if to welcome them. Michael got in and Ivan followed. Abraham stood examining the automobile wondering what in the world this could be. He leaned down cautiously and put a foot in the car and used the handle on the roof to slide in. The padded, black leather seats were incredibly comfortable and seemed to be heating themselves.

"It's mesmerizing isn't it? The city..." Michael said.

"I've never seen anything like it," Abraham said, staring out the window as the door finished shutting.

"Ivan mentioned that you'd been away for a while. I'm curious what for, if that's alright?"

Abraham broke his eye contact with the city and gave Michael his attention, hesitant to answer.

"Murder," he replied ashamed, waiting for their reaction.

"Well you'll fit right in then." Michael laughed, and as he laughed Abraham felt his heart sink for fear of what was to come.

"So what time should I send a car to get you two in the morning to come by the office? Autopilot, St. Peters Street, plot 9 building 8."

The car started, moving slow at first, but as they pulled out of the circle they started gaining speed fast.

"Why don't you send it around 10? We're probably going to sleep in some," Ivan answered.

Abraham returned his gaze to the city, too awestricken to want to speak. The car turned onto one of the on ramps that led to the suspended highways, which were so close to the tops of buildings it looked almost like the on ramp was coming out of one of the buildings itself. Abraham felt his stomach drop from gravity as they rode higher and higher. The city was flying by, turning nearby structures into blurs of color, almost as things had on the train but not quite as bad, so as Abraham could still make out things in the distance. It was hard to see much with all the lights blurring though, so Abraham turned back toward Ivan and Michael who had been reacquainting themselves after so long.

"How do you like the car?" Michael asked Abraham, grinning, already knowing the answer to his question.

"It's definitely different" Abraham stated, looking the car over again and politely returning the smile. Abraham didn't know what to make of him. He seemed nice enough but most do at first for that matter.

After riding awhile the car pulled up to a large building, not as decorative or tall as the ones by the station but they still looked grander than anything Abraham had ever seen. On either side of the street they were surrounded by similar looking buildings; short but very wide with the old rectangular architecture, all with lots of windows and a small balcony overlooking the street. The car doors opened as they had before and Abraham stepped out into the street, still at a loss for words over the mindfulness of the vehicle. It was a residential neighborhood; apartment buildings seemed to be the only thing around. There were no stores or even houses, only the grand apartment buildings, almost forming their own little community. Over the tops of the apartments he could see the huge oval skyscrapers of the city, all more or less centered near the same area with the thin highway twisting and curving all around them. As he stood beside the car waiting, he noticed a second car pull up behind them. Michael's bodyguards stepped out, but didn't proceed to walk any closer to them.

"Let me show you guys around your apartment real quick," Michael said, as he and Ivan walked past Abraham. They walked up the entry stairs and Michael pressed his thumb against a screen beside the glass doors to the building. A thin blue line of light scanned the thumb and the glass doors opened for them. Abraham followed them inside. The lobby of the building was a clean dull area, that didn't have too much to it except a couple paintings and some flowers here and there. The building was carelessly trying to create the homey feeling for its residents. Michael went over to a computer screen and activated it by scanning his thumb again.

"Grant Access" he stated clearly to the computer.

The computer projected a hologram into the air. It was a young pretty woman with blonde hair, so real Abraham could have reached out and touched her.

"What do you wish to do?" she asked in a similarly authentic voice.

"I want to give these two men all access to the flat," Michael said.

"Scan your thumbs," The hologram responded.

Michael gestured for Ivan and Abraham to go up and scan their thumbs. Abraham hesitantly placed his against the screen along with Ivan. The blue line moved from the top of the screen to the bottom and then quietly beeped signaling that it was finished.

"Thank you. Do you wish to change the billing information Michael?"

"No thanks, that's all," Michael responded.

The computer stopped projecting the woman and she disappeared back inside the computer. "Those are your keys to the building and your flat now if you were wondering what was going on Abraham, so try not to get your thumb cut off." Michael laughed, but something in his tone made Abraham think he was only half joking. Michael led them down a hallway on the right until they reached a glass cylinder held together by metal frames, which slide open quickly once they were within a few feet.

"Fourth," Michael said once they had all gotten in.

The doors shut and almost instantly they reopened on the fourth floor, after giving off a feeling of nausea as they sped away from the ground and gravity attempted to pull them back. Abraham followed Ivan and Michael out of the elevator and before them was a lobby with four hallways extending from it. At the far wall across from the elevator was a stand with blue flowers on it and paintings on both sides. One painting was a grassy meadow with pink flowers and the other was a woman with blonde hair, much like the hologram from the computer. She was crying in the picture and wearing the same shade of blue as the flowers below her on the stand. It was a sad scene even though the decorators had probably only picked the arrangement because of the color of the woman's dress, which matched the flowers and the sky in the painting of the meadow, ignoring that it might have been in bad taste from the conflicting emotions. Michael led them down a hallway to the left of the flowers and stopped at a light brown door near the end of the hallway.

"Here it is. All you have to do is put your hand on the door and push. The computer systems made a mask of your hand so it already has your hand print. Just push on the door and it'll open for you, easy enough."

Ivan placed his hand on the door and pushed lightly. The lock clicked and the door opened slowly. Abraham followed Ivan in after Michael. The apartment was very nice; black tiled floors, with pale white walls and furniture to match. The kitchen was on the right as soon as they walked in and was partly connected to the living room through a small window above the sink. The living room, as well as the other rooms, had a circular architecture to it. White leather couches in the center, facing a circular projector attached to a bending support beam hanging from the ceiling. At the center of the projector was an electric looking blue light, providing curiosity as to what it was. All along the back wall of the living room was a raised platform with a fireplace over to the right. Michael went over to the wall beside the projector and motioned his hand. The back wall suddenly changed to glass and Abraham found himself staring out over the lit up night of the city.

"Amazing what technology can do now-a-days," Michael said earnestly, staring down at the city.

"We'll this is it then. If you want to watch TV just stare at the projector and say on. From there just use your hands to change the channel or turn the volume up or down," he said motioning from side to side then from up to down.

"I'd better be going. We got a big day tomorrow so get your rest. If you're hungry..." He said walking over to the kitchen area. "...food's in here and in the cabinets," he said opening a large metallic oval with two doors and then waving his hand across the wall and a small square opened up revealing several pantry items.

"I'll see you boys tomorrow, have a good night." He smiled, giving Ivan one last hug and shaking Abraham's hand. With that, he walked out shutting the door behind him.

"Lot to take in," Ivan acknowledged jokingly, sounding exhausted. "Can't even imagine how you feel" he smiled. "I think I'm going to go to bed but you should look around. Maybe watch some TV. That'll help you more than anything I think, just seeing what the rest of the world looks like." He nodded at Abraham and walked out of the living room toward one of the rooms on the left.

Abraham stood there for a few minutes and then walked over to the couch and sat down. It was a lot to take in. He couldn't believe how much things had changed. It was frightening how far behind Abraham felt, compared to everything. It was hard to know what to think. He got back on his feet and walked over to the wall and waved his hand changing the window back into a wall, and then he rehanged it back into the glass window, and stared out over the city. The city, Michael, his new job, and the past few days were running through his mind. It would be impossible for him to sleep tonight though he had felt as if he was dreaming since they had arrived, as though he had never woken up and was still sleeping on the train. It was overwhelming but Abraham hadn't felt as excited about anything in a long time, but maybe it was just his nerves. He had become filled with hope and whether it was real or just an illusion brought on by the city, he was curious to find out what the future held for him.

Chapter 8

Abraham woke the next morning half expecting everything from the night before to be a dream. He laid there in the bed that had been waiting for him and tried to remember a time he had been as comfortable. The burgundy sheets were soft against his rough skin and the bed had a self-monitoring system, always keeping the bed a constant temperature in regard to Abraham's body temperature. He played with the windows as he laid there looking out over the city absent mindedly. Waving his hand, turning the projector on giving him a pearly white wall, and then waving his hand again to turn the projector off, revealing the windows. The morning sun shone down upon the city, glaring off of skyscrapers and the metal frames of the highways. Abraham had never seen such a beautiful city. It inspired something in him, and as much as he wanted to chase after those inspirations, he had no idea what they were for. They were just there, stirring up excitement in him and giving him a reason to get out of bed that morning.

After spending about an hour figuring out how the pulse activated shower worked, he dressed himself in one of the soft black suits that were waiting for him in the closet, and walked out into the living room, finding Ivan there sitting on the couch, watching television.

"Hey, so how do you like it so far?" he asked smiling.

"It's nice; never lived anywhere this nice."

"Me neither, I told Michael it didn't have to be the best, but obviously he didn't listen."

Abraham nodded and walked into the kitchen to make himself a drink.

"Where are the glasses at?" He asked, realizing that Michael had not told them where any sort of dishes were.

"They're right beside the fridge, just reach for them and the wall will disappear... A lot of holograms in this city, but I guess it's supposed to be the big new thing, not having to touch anything."

Abraham reached at the wall beside the fridge and suddenly the wall disappeared revealing several different kinds of glasses. He grabbed a plain cylindrical one and filled it with clear water from the faucet, the glass cooling his hand as the cold water poured into it.

"The car should be here any minute. Michael had just called before you came in," Ivan explained.

Abraham finished his drink, setting the glass on the counter beside the sink and then walked over and sat on the couch perpendicular of Ivan's. The news was on and Abraham lost himself with admiring the scenery the reporter was in, hardly paying attention to her words. It was almost as if he was watching one of the sci-fi films from his childhood, as alien as things looked. Maybe ten minutes later Ivan got a call from someone saying that the car was out front, so they left the apartment and headed downstairs. As they were driven to Michaels "Company" as he called it, Abraham couldn't help but notice how concentrated the city was. He hadn't noticed in the dark last night, but today it was clear how the majority of tall buildings and corporations were in the center of the city. On the outskirts of the city, particularly in the west and north, it was mainly huge homesteads, probably built for CEO's and city officials.

Michaels building was a little on the outskirts of where the biggest concentration of skyscrapers were only reaching about three tenths of their height. It was about five stories tall and like most of the other buildings, it was almost completely built of spotless glass, with a steel metal framing. The building was also on an incline within the city, so it had white stone stairs leading up to the building with railings on either side, and there was a small garden of mostly white lotuses on both sides of the doors. A young lady in a light gray suit met them at the doors and then escorted them up to see Michael on the fifth floor. It appeared a lot more legitimate than Ivan had let on. At a glance it all looked like any other business. Apparently at one point Michael had been completely legitimate, but after becoming disgruntled over the small profits of his company, and perhaps boredom with the quiet life, he had decided to start a more risky venture. He still produced and marketed new items on the legitimate side of his business, being too much of a coward to go completely illegal, though the real money he made was through his rackets, the most profitable now being the selling of genetics. Michael had thought it all through, or so he told Ivan and Abraham. Ivan had probably heard it before but he sat and listened quietly anyways with convincing interest.

As they talked over the lunch that Michael had laid out for them Abraham began to understand what exactly his and Ivan's new jobs would entail. Michael had the genes he sold made in the very building they were in. There was a laboratory on the third floor where the "out of-work" scientists that Michael had recruited (or blackmailed) from various places around the providence, would transform samples of DNA by recombining the strand of genome, and hopefully finding a code that successfully altered a strand. Out of the entire human genome 80 percent actually contribute while the other twenty percent are just dead weight. The only reason they are in the genome is because they are more likely to make copies of themselves than other genes that "didn't make the evolutionary cut". Michael told them that what the scientists do is they cut out some of the twenty percent and replace them with other chromosomes to have an effect on the body giving the host more strength, better resistance to diseases, and various other genetic modifications. He must have wanted to be more of a biologist from the excitement he had about it when he told them. After they had a combination of a gene that didn't kill the host or fail to change the hosts DNA, they would package it and find a buyer. They supply the people of the city with a cost effective way for getting genetic modifications. Getting them from physicians was incredibly expensive due to the availability of certain genes and who actually needed them. Apparently it was a pretty thorough process to see whether or not someone even applied to get genetic modifications, based on family history and societal status, etc. It was one of the main reasons contributing to the homeless people around the city not being able to be hired, because people with genetic modifications were the better candidate for the job. After all why would you settle for the less qualified person? Some legitimate companies even bought from Michael, mostly for produce but occasionally it would be for an employee. All Ivan and Abraham would be doing is accompanying him on the sales and collecting payments. A lot like errand boys. Michael really made it out to be an effortless job, though only a fool would believe him. Ivan had already told Abraham that he sold to everyone, rich and poor, which probably caused more problems than it was worth, but Michael had built himself an empire in spite of it. Michael seemed as though he could talk forever, but thankfully Ivan suggested that they go back to the apartment and rest for the night that Michael had planned for them. He must have been getting bored listening to the same story.

Abraham was still getting ready for the night, when he heard Ivan through the apartment shouting that the car would be there in 10 minutes. Once they'd gotten back from Michaels facility Abraham had just laid in bed for the longest time. It was ironic that he would do the only thing he'd been able to do in prison now that he was free, but as comfortable as the bed was, it was a hard thing to resist. The sheets were the smoothest silk and the pillows were so soft, it felt as though Abraham was resting his head on a cloud. He would drift back and forth from consciousness, lazily wasting the remainder of the day away until he had to start getting ready for the night. He finished tying his shoes and stood up to admire himself in the mirror. He still looked malnourished but at least he was starting to improve. Compared to now, he must have looked like a skeleton during his time at the prison. However, the suits Michael had bought him took the attention away from the unappealing bony curves of his body. Sleek black with a satin red shirt beneath the jacket; the best clothes he'd ever worn. His hair was still somewhat buzzed from the training camp but it looked nice enough.

He walked out of his room, his shoes enhancing the sound of his steps as he walked along the black marble floor of his room. Ivan was standing in the living room leaning on the couch and gazing at a hologram being displayed from his wrist. From what Ivan had explained earlier that day on the way to Michaels that was what phones had turned into; computer like devices being projected from a band on the wrist looking a bit like a watch. Just tapping the little rectangle in the golden or silver band turned on the device, projecting a screen with several options. It was not an easy device to use for someone who had only known phones that were attached to the wall by a cord, so Abraham hoped he would not have to use the silver banded one Michael gave him very often. Ivan looked up acknowledging that Abraham had just walked into the room and then his attention went back to the hologram.

"I think he's here. Just a second..." He said as he finished what he was doing.

He tapped the rectangle on his wrist, retracting the hologram and then stood to his feet and led the way out. Down on the street waiting was Michael's narrow white car with black tinted windows and as Ivan and Abraham walked out the entrance of their apartment, the vehicle's doors opened automatically, much as they had been doing, but it was beginning to become a little unsettling for Abraham. The fact that the machine was doing this all on its own and no human was involved made Abraham hesitant to embrace the technology. Abraham slid into the car beside Ivan, noticing that Michael was sitting across from them wearing the same dark grey suit he'd been wearing earlier that day.

"Which one are we going to?" Ivan asked getting adjusted in his seat.

"I was thinking Atmosphere, but it's your first night back in the city so it's up to you. It'd even been a year before you went to prison since I'd seen you."

"Atmosphere's fine," Ivan said smiling.

"Sounds good; I've already set us up a table anyways." Michael had probably been planning to go to Atmosphere regardless.

Ivan and Michael reminisced on the way to the club and Abraham watched the city as they went, not having much to contribute to the conversation. It was a hard conversation for him to relate to anyways, it being about what had happened to this or that or new buildings and stories of things that had happened to them. Occasionally they would try to include Abraham in the conversation but Abraham didn't commit; only nodding his head or one word answers. The night sky was lit up again much like the night before, except tonight there were a few clouds out reflecting some of the cities glow. They were taking the road they had taken from the station to their apartment from what it looked like; Abraham having seen some familiar looking buildings.

It seemed as though they were headed toward the heart of the city from the way it emitted light from every direction, as if beckoning people to it. It was the warm center of the universe, where everyone wanted to be. As they drove Abraham saw the tall skyscrapers from earlier that day. At night the skyscrapers had a dull glow about them, coming from the occasional light on in an office and the electric blue or neon green lights lining the frames of the building, mostly to warn low flying aircraft. As they drew further and further into the light, Abraham began making out ads for drinks and videos of people dancing and singing being projected into the sky and off buildings. He also began feeling a vibration building itself up as they came closer.

Then it became a hum that slowly transformed into electric beats that exploded and bounced back to a high screeching noise, and various other rhythms all seemingly shaking the very earth. It was surprising to hear, never being able to predict where the beat of the song would go next. The majority of the music Abraham had heard had been orchestral or string. What instrument had made this was a mystery to him but it fit well with the city, almost adding to the overall complexion. The lights in some of the lively clubs they were starting to pass would flash in beat with the music, making the scene appear to be fast forwarding mechanically from the darkness in-between. Even in the dark you could make out some of the people because of the neon necklaces, and clothes, and tattoos they had would glow brightly. It was intimidating, but Abraham couldn't take his eyes off of what he was seeing. Many of the clubs at street level had glass walls revealing the activity within; people dancing and attempting to yell over the music. Alcohol and drugs were prominent as well in the majority of the clubs, people indulging in various drinks and powders laid out over their tables. The car kept moving though, further into the light. The clubs seemed to get more private as they went on, the emergence of waiting lines and guards altering the feeling of the area. Not as many of the buildings had glass walls, and most were elevated, with steps and carpet leading majestically up to them now as well.

Finally the car stopped in front of a huge building with large intricately designed fountains on either side of the entrance and white flowered vines crawling up the doorway. The people outside waiting to get in were innumerable, all being pushed back by the muscular guards at the front, blocking the doorway. The doors of the car opened, immersing them in the scent of musk and perfume, along with the less sweet smell of alcohol and sweat. As Abraham stepped out, he stared at the area in which he found himself, completing a full circle around, staring at all the buildings and their fluorescent signs accompanied by holographic advertisements, unable to believe the atmosphere in which he found himself. Looking in some of the long windows near the tops of the clubs where the richest most powerful men of the city sat and smoked cigars discussing politics and watching as everyone at the street level drunkenly stumbled here and there, as if they were looking after their very own property.

Abraham followed Ivan and Michael up the stone stairs toward the building with a huge fluorescent white sign with the word "Atmosphere" written creatively on it. The front was a large cylindrical building that was connected on the far right of a large oval building, with balconies on every level. They walked past the large crowd of people and when they reached the doorway Michael nodded and smiled at the guards as they opened the white leather doors for him and let the three of them pass through. They walked in the darkly blue lit hallway toward the rest of the club and once they made it out into the opening Abraham saw just how vast the place was. There were close to 6 stories, each was lit some fluorescent red or green or blue color, with large bars at the center and beautiful women in skimpy clothes dancing on random little stages all around. There were light beams racing across the floors and walls as well, and the very floor tiles they walked on lit up in a metallic black as if to make them feel as though the very steps they took influenced the solidity of the club, turning the floor to liquid as they walked. Abraham had felt anxious about the whole thing and was getting more nervous about being here, the sick feeling in his stomach growing as they walked. Michael led them up a couple of floors on winding staircases scattered throughout the layout, greeting various people as he went. He was a popular guy it seemed, or at least made it look that way. He finally walked over to a crescent moon booth toward the back, that over looked the rest of the club from a raised platform in the corner. The floor on the level was a dark burgundy carpet, matching the lighting of that particular floor and distinguishing it from the other black tiled floors with metallic black colored walls. His suit matched at least,

Abraham joked to himself nervously as he noticed the red and black coloring of his surroundings. They walked up to the booth and the men and women currently there stood up to greet the three of them, drunkenly laughing, happy at their arrival, and clearing way for the men to sit as well. After introductions, Abraham took a seat across from Ivan and Michael, next to a lovely blonde girl in a shimmering blue dress. Her perfume was intoxicating and making him even more nervous in his present situation. It'd been a long time since he'd seen a woman and the more he sat by her, the more he wanted to stare at her for the same reason one might stare at a cloud, but he resisted the notion and nervously looked from place to place around the club, trying to hide his anxiety. Everyone seemed to have lost all cares in the world, if they had even had any, and were overcome by their narrow minded mindset of pleasure. Abraham just smiled politely during the conversations that were being shared. He could hardly hear anything anyway. A waitress came over bringing them all drinks and set the tray of glowing green ooze at the center of the table. Everyone took one, as did Abraham, and followed Michael's position as he prepared to toast.

"To my brother returning, and our new friend Abraham! Cheers!" Michael said which was repeated by the guests at the table. It was oddly cold to the touch and the taste was a mixture of fruit and heavy alcohol as well as something else he couldn't quite match, differing from the toxic substance Abraham had thought they were ingesting. Whatever the mysterious booze was, he felt at ease almost instantly, the nervous anxiety becoming such a stranger to him that he couldn't even understand why he had felt that way in the first place.

"Only the best" Michael said looking at Abraham, as he laughed. Abraham laughed and nodded, agreeing on the toxic looking alcohol to Michael's content.

They were there for a while, talking and laughing, enjoying the night. Abraham was more attentive to the conversation and people at the table, feeling more relaxed now than he had been. He could be drunk but at the moment he felt in too good of spirits to try and ruin it with analysis. People would stop by and hug Ivan or joke with Michael frequently before moving on to some other part of the club. Ivan sat across from Abraham, blatantly getting drunk and was in a flirtatious mood with a woman that had beautiful oak hair next to him. One of the men apparently was a client of Michaels and a couple of the women were or had been as well, from what Abraham had gathered through the conversations going about the table. Others had worked with Michael and one of the women was even with Ivan before he left the city and was at the moment stealing jealous glances at the woman he was flirting with. The night went on happily like this for quite a while. But like a spring frost over newly grown flowers, Abraham saw a man walking up toward the booth with a fowl look on his face. He was the only one in the club who had looked as though he were there for other purposes than pure pleasure. He walked up to Michael quickly and leaned across the table impatiently shouting over the music.

"I want my money back Michael! I still had some time left before I had to pay you. That money was for someone else, so now I'm in deep shit unless I get that back!"

"Well you should have thought about your other debts before you decided to make a deal with me," Michael said passively smiling as if the man had been joking.

The other man's face instantly scowled seeing how lightly Michael had taken him.

"No, you said I had three more days till I had to pay you!" he shouted pointing at the table as if on it laid the very agreement that they had come to.

"I changed my mind. It's not hard to see why with what you owe to everyone else around here. Now if you don't get out of my face, I'm going to make sure that next time my boys don't just take the money you owe me. Now leave us alone or you'll wish you had!" Michael said coolly, finally showing the situation the respect it deserved.

A look of defeat passed over the man's face as he realized he was going to make no progress. He glanced over everyone at the table before leaving and his gaze fixed on Ivan. He looked as though he'd seen a ghost. Ivan glared back at him in recognition, taking the large cigar out of his mouth and blowing the smoke into the nightclubs already mixed odor.

"I'd heard you were back in town. Funny, didn't realize your sentence was so short," The man finally said sounding sarcastic as he backed away.

"Good behavior" Ivan said dryly joking as he spewed smoke from his mouth again.

The man glared at him and finally turned around and left. After a few minutes Michael stood up and started walking away from the group.

"What the hell was that about?" he directed at Ivan as he went.

Ivan hurried up and walked over to Michael out of earshot. Abraham watched them curiously as the rest of their company began whispering to one another and laughing at the tension of the situation. Ivan was explaining something desperately and Michael was glancing between the floor and Ivan taking in the story, revealing nothing of his thoughts. Michael started talking and Ivan just nodded. After they had concluded the conversation everyone tried acting like the man had never came, but the mood had shifted some and was no longer in as high spirits. The conversations weren't quite as humorous and full of laughter as before.

After drinking a little more the three men said goodnight to their party and began the decent to the base level of the club. The building was still very much alive, even though the excitement in their party had died. On the outside there was surprisingly still a massive amount of people trying to get in as late as it was. There were even people being dragged off by police as well because they had passed out waiting to get into the nightclub.

"You guys go ahead and head back in my car; I have to go handle something over at "The Decedents" club. Michael said with an air of suspicion about his tone.

"It's good to have you back brother and make sure you take care of that problem," he said as he hugged Ivan.

"Have a good night boys" and with that he started walking off to the right accompanied by one of the men that had sat with them at the booth.

The two men stepped into the car which had oddly been waiting for them as they walked out of the building. On the way back to their flat Abraham was sitting across from Ivan wondering what was going on. Ivan was hunched over staring at the ground, sweating from the alcohol. He lifted his head up and looked at Abraham.

"That guy's one of the reasons I went away."

"He was with me when we went to steal the heroin. Turns out the feds had been tracking the heroin and when we were caught he made a deal to get less time. Put me and my cousin away for a long time." Ivan paused staring at the ground.

"He must have jumped town after his sentence but Michaels worried that he'll try and blackmail us, threatening to tell the police about my situation." He took a deep breath and cleared his throat, wiping the sweat from the right side of his face.

"So... we'll kill him," he said slowly and looked back up at Abraham, studying him to see any sign of resentment but Abraham stared indifferently and listened.

"I'll handle most of it, I just need you there as backup. I don't even think I'll need you, but Michael wanted you to come along, make sure things went smoothly." Ivan was bobbing his head as if he was agreeing with something.

"Ok. When are we going?" Abraham asked trying not to sound like he was thinking too hard about it, though that was a lie.

"We'll do it first thing in the morning. I'll get you up. Doubt I'll sleep much tonight," Ivan said straitening his spin and relaxing against the back of the seat.

It was one thing after another. No time for adjustment but maybe that was a good thing. Abraham compared it to wading through uncomfortably cold water and then fully submerging yourself to rid the body of the uneven feeling. Abraham was being thrown into his new life instead of taking it in strides, which would hopefully just require him to adjust quicker. Until he adjusted though, everything would feel like a dream on the verge of waking.

He tried not to think about his past at all. It was the only way he could block any of those feelings of displacement out.

Abraham woke to Ivan knocking on his door telling him it was time to wake up. He rubbed his eyes, trying to cease the bulging pressure of his head. Memories from the night before flooded back to him, adding to his discomfort. From the way Ivan's voice had fluttered, Abraham could tell how anxious he was for the morning to be over. Abraham sat up and put his feet to the cold marble. He didn't bother showering today. He'd only have to come back and get cleaned up again anyway. As he dressed himself, the unsettled feeling in his gut increased. Even though he wouldn't have minded dying, not even a week ago, the city had inspired in him a desire for survival, and knowing that the events of the day may lead him to his death, made a nauseous feeling grow in his stomach as he clutched to life.

He finished putting on another of his suits, which was what Michael apparently desired them to wear even in situations such as this, and went out into the living room to meet Ivan who was looking out the giant window, deep in thought. He heard Abraham approach and turned to walk toward him quickly. There were two pistols on the small coffee table adjacent to the intersection of the perpendicular couches and as he walked over he picked one up and threw it toward Abraham as if it were a ball. Abraham caught it startled, feeling the cold metal weight of the gun.

"Don't worry, the safety's on" He said seeing Abraham's surprise.

He picked the other one up and put it in his belt behind him.

"You probably won't even have to use it, but just to be safe. I'm sure you remember from the training we got right?"

"Yea, I remember" Abraham said staring at the gun as if in some sort of trance and recalling what had been drilled into his head just a couple of months ago.

The feeling in his stomach had spread and grew like a disease, gaining girth and now it felt as though his heart was in his mouth. Hopefully he would calm down when it was time to act or his new life would be short lived.

"Let's go then, Michael's told me where we'll find him, so let's hope he's actually there," Ivan declared half-heartedly and he hastily walked out the door.

Abraham put the pistol in his belt and followed Ivan shutting the door behind them.

The car ride was silent, both concentrating intensely on the situation. Ivan was staring at the ground and Abraham at his hands, which he rested, clenched tightly on his thighs. He'd never done anything like this. The waiting was going to kill him before any sort of gun even had the chance. When he was in the army he'd been thrown into the fighting and he had had to act without having the time to think about what the consequences of failing were. But in this situation it seemed like he had an eternity to think about what was going to happen and what death or failure would mean for him. The car stopped and with it Abraham's heart stopped. He looked up jerkily through the window. They were at a warehouse on the outskirts of town, judging from how far away the skyscrapers looked. There were old factories and warehouses all around them as well as a couple of broken down apartment buildings. They anxiously stepped out of the car.

"Okay, just back me up in here." Ivan directed him.

They hurried over to a small doorway on the side of one of the factories. Ivan stood on one side of the doorway and Abraham shuffled over to the other side, drawing his gun and waiting for Ivan. Ivan pulled his gun out and got ready. He took several deep breaths and looked Abraham intensely in the eyes as if asking if Abraham were ready. He took Abraham's answer and moved to face the door, and lifted his foot stomping forcefully through the door by its handle. The door flew open and Ivan and Abraham ran inside. The man from last night was there, along with several other men who fled through a back doorway into the manufacturing area, as the two of them invaded the large office. Ivan fired several shots at the man from the night before, hitting him and sending him to the floor. Abraham, seeing Ivan's actions aimed and shot at the men leaving, but he was too late, his shots hitting the door frame as they ran through. "Stay here and make sure no one doubles back!" Ivan shouted running after the men who'd gotten away. Abraham stood in the middle of the room anxiously moving. There were stacks of money on a table near the right corner of the room, opposite the doorway that Ivan had just ran through. It was hard to believe that with all this money the man couldn't have paid Michael and whoever else off. Abraham was surprised at how calm he was. He was shaking, but he'd only mistaken his adrenaline for nerves. He looked over at the man scrounging on the cement of the office. He had several bullet wounds in his chest and was now lying in a pool of his own blood. He let out a bloody cough, spewing it over the floor in front of him as he strained to see his condition.

"Fuck" he cried out grasping his chest in pain.

"You fucking cocksuckers!" He shouted, but Abraham ignored him and glanced around anxiously, thinking he'd heard something from the doorway Ivan had just gone through.

"Oh, shit" He let out painfully, almost in tears.

"I should have known. I should have known that untrustworthy fuck would do this to me." Abraham looked at the man for a second before averting his eyes, but in that second their eyes had met.

"Who the hell are you anyways?!" the man coughed out inquisitively.

"Some thug Michael picked up off the street...no, no you're a friend of Ivan's aren't you, you stupid fuck." The man insulted, flinching in pain.

"He'll just use you to prevent himself from going down when the time comes." Abraham made the mistake of looking at the man again, provoking him more.

"He did it to me and his own fucking cousin, what makes you think that he's not going to fuck you also!" the man screamed, angrily recounting the past.

Abraham was taken aback.

"What are you talking about?" he asked cautiously

"Ooh." The man laughed coughing up blood. Abraham could tell the man didn't have much longer. "So now you're interested? Ivan's one selfish son-of-a-bitch. If it's convenient for him, he'll do whatever it takes for his own self-preservation." The man's chest lifted and fell more rapidly now.

"If he gave his own cousin up to the feds then he won't think twice about giving you to them," he threatened, coughing up blood occasionally.

Abraham hurried over to him, dropping to his knees and grabbing the man's collar with his free hand, choking him a little.

"What do you mean?" Abraham demanded irritated at the man's evasiveness.

The man smiled back at him and coughed up more blood, some of it splattering on Abraham's hand. The light in his brown eyes was fading. Abraham wouldn't have time to figure out what the man was talking about, if any of it was even true. He dropped the man and got up off of his knee. What was he talking about? The man very well could have just been trying to corrupt Abraham, but Abraham had let his guard down since coming to the city. Was Ivan lying to him? Ivan had only approached him at the training camp because he didn't think he could escape alone. What if Abraham had just been Ivan's insurance, and when the time came Ivan would have just used Abraham to get away? He heard footsteps running to the doorway. He raised his gun toward the door, ready to shoot. Ivan ran through it but fell against the wall with his hands up when he saw Abraham holding the gun at him. Abraham pulled it back.

"What happened?" he asked, hiding his thoughts.

"I got one but the other was too fast and got away. Fuck him, we got this slimy bastard," he huffed agitatedly recovering himself and kicking the body of the man.

He started walking toward the door they had burst through. "It's fine though, they didn't know who I am. We're done here."

"You don't want to take that money?" Abraham asked curiously.

"No, if we take that then whoever it belongs to will just be asking about it and the last thing we need is a problem with the mob. Come on, let's go."

Abraham followed him out of the warehouse and they stepped into the car to leave. Ivan was still breathing hard from the chase, as they began to head back to the apartment. "Holy shit" Ivan laughed excitedly, the adrenaline still pumping through his veins. Abraham smiled back at him ingenuinely. He thought about asking Ivan what the man had said but decided against it. If it was true then the last thing he would want to do would be to tell Ivan he knew. Perhaps the man had just been trying to manipulate him as well though. He looked out the window and watched as the sun flew higher and higher into the sky as they were driven back to their apartment. Abraham looked out over the city from the highways. It was interesting how the skyscrapers shadows projected a shadow which covered a sixth of the city in shadow during the morning and afternoon. Only at midday was the shadow cast on itself. Thus the city was divided between those who were truly in the shadow and those that were only walking through the shadow to the light.

Chapter 9

The months passed slowly and eventually Abraham began to feel more at ease. He'd had no problems with Ivan or Michael regardless of his suspicions, but he was still curious what the man had said with his dying breath. He passed the days and weeks doing odd jobs for Michael; typically collecting money or making deals but the consistent hollowness he'd began to feel was weighing on him. It was a cold, sunny morning, after a cool rain, and he and Ivan were sitting at a café a couple blocks from their apartment eating breakfast. It was an older part of town and was bare of the progressively annoying holo-advertisements seen all throughout the city, which is some of what held its appeal for the two men. Their peevish waitress was a pretty, young girl and Ivan had been making her blush all morning. She had brought them an order of eggs and coffee and they sat there eating breakfast and watching the world around them move with the passing of the sun. It seemed as if they were on the outside of something. Like they knew something that no one else did and as people interacted with the world, Abraham and Ivan sat and watched them, as if they were judging their every move.

The waitress walked up; "Can I get you boys anything else?" she asked, her eyes glowing at Ivan, but trying to be fair.

Abraham smiled, finding her demeanor funny.

"No thanks doll," Ivan said smirking and handing her his credit chit.

Her face lit up red, provoking her small dimples as she grinned at him giggling shyly but then she turned to walk away embarrassed. Ivan's phone started ringing.

"What's up?" he answered dully, still looking after the young girl.

It must have been Michael from the bland greeting.

"Alright, we've just finished breakfast. We'll be there as soon as we can." He hung up and then sent a message to one of Michael's cars to come pick them up.

Neither of them had driven since they'd come to the city, which Abraham found disturbing just how little anyone drove anymore, the roads being controlled by "smart" cars as they were called. It was hard for people to cope with the suspended driving on the highways for which the auto-driving cars were made, only adding to people's disengagement with the surrounding world.

"Michael wants us to come pick up a supply and go drop it off east of town for some livestock company" Ivan eventually said unenthusiastically, Abraham nodded acknowledgingly.

The waitress was back and extended her hand to give Ivan the credit chit, seeming to have composed herself over her short absence. Ivan took the card and when she turned to leave, he gently grabbed her wrist and pulled her back flirtatiously.

"Just in case" he said sliding a card into her hand.

She looked at it stiffening and smiled wide, girlishly giggling again.

The two prisoners stood up and started walking toward the direction the car was coming from. It was turning into a nice day out. Not as cold as when they had first come to town, but not hot either and the rain from the night before had given everything a renewed look as if washing away all the contamination that had collected. Few clouds in the sky, but they only helped the fresh feeling of the morning. As they walked along Abraham noticed a homeless family lying in some garbage still damp from the night.

Weeks ago Ivan had explained to Abraham his disgust for the businesses around town because they were directly responsible for the current economic inequality. He couldn't believe how there could be people lying in the gutter, dirty and starving, when there was plenty of food and wealth. After eugenics came about the population went down considerably and suddenly there was hardly any recorded starvation but from what Ivan had said, the businesses had just horded the resources giving jobs to people that they considered better than others and genetics only made it harder for the poor people of the city to get jobs as expensive as genetics were. All the factory jobs now being done mostly by machines left the poor only a handful of jobs, which were quickly filled, and the rest of the population were given to the streets and other harsh outlets. The poor children of the city didn't have much of a future ahead of them and the cruelty of life was that they never had a chance to begin with. Apparently officials didn't like seeing this either though because they'd been trying to get a law passed for the sterilization of everyone who didn't have genetic modifications in their family's genealogy. And when there is a market, there is business to be done, thus the reason for Michael's new found product. Where the ethics of life had gone, Abraham did not know. Ivan truly believed they were helping people, and to an extent Abraham felt that way too. But when someone missed a payment and Abraham or Ivan had to go take care of it, it was hard to feel that way.

Their ride took a left onto the street they were walking beside and pulled next to the sidewalk for them to get in. Once they arrived at Michaels' they went up to his office to see him. He was sitting at his desk along with several of his thugs standing around the office.

"Hey, bout time you guys got here" he said as if he had been waiting all day on them.

"I need you guys to accompany these boys down under a bridge to the east flats and oversee the deal. These guys know most of the specifics; just make sure nothing goes wrong," he said lighting a large cigar.

"Come back here after you're done," he said as he was blowing out smoke, smelling the room of a heavy smoky smell and then turning his gaze to his phone, pre-occupied with some other matter.

They followed the other men down to where the cars were parked in a half moon drive and stepped into one of the cars they had. There were three cars altogether with two men to a car. Ivan and Abraham got into the middle one and the convoy started off.

"Must have a lot on his mind today" Ivan stated, thinking about how distant Michael had seemed.

Abraham nodded remembering the hollow look Michael had had as they walked into his office. The spot Michael had chosen was under a bridge that was about twenty feet above the starved dirt from which a dried up river had once flowed through. It was an unusual spot compared to the company warehouses they usually went to for this sort of exchange, but Michael had insisted that they do business elsewhere so that he didn't start attracting to much attention. When they arrived the buyers were already out of their cars waiting. They were young for what Abraham had expected and most had pistols on them except for a few. Abraham stepped out of the car, putting on a pair of black sunglass to shade the glare of the sun, and motioned for the men to get the suitcases out of the trunk and bring them over to the buyers. The sun had come out through the course of the day and was exceptionally bright in contrast to the dreary gray morning. From what he gathered he wouldn't be involved much by how clear cut the deal seemed. He pulled out a cigarette and proceeded to light it as he leaned against the car that had driven him and Ivan.

He sat there and watched from a distance as the business commenced, blowing out smoke to his left to avoid it being blown back into his face by the wind. Ivan was off talking to one of the men that had come with them, inquiring into the reason for Michael's strange demeanor;

something to do with the mayors re-election apparently. Abraham stared off into the wilderness, away from the city which cut off abruptly into a thin forest. It was the farthest outside the city he'd been since arriving. It was enticing to see its calm beauty again, the trees rustling in the wind with tiny birds gliding playfully from tree to tree. The leaves were as green as Abraham could remember ever seeing leaves, and full of life unlike the decayed leaves of the forest during his time in the army. As if to ruin the beauty of nature, loud blasts echoed and before he knew what was happening someone grabbed him from behind and brought him to the ground, as a gun shot went off ahead of him. He jerked his head to see who had grabbed him, panicking in the confusion. It was Ivan, who was pulling his pistol out quickly and positioning himself against the car for cover. Abraham crawled further toward the back of the car where Ivan was, trying to recompose himself after the surprising shock of the situation. Bullets rang out from all around as they put holes in the car; some were even exploding into the ground around where Abraham was crawling, specs of dried dirt hitting him in the face after impact. Ivan ripped open the back car door and they both hurried in. Abraham's heart was racing as he pushed himself against the seat trying to avoid exploding glass. Ivan shut the door and shouted at the car to get moving.

"What happened?" Abraham shouted as they began speeding away.

"It was a set up! These guys were supposed to be from an animal engineering corporation but I don't think they were the guys we were supposed to be meeting," Ivan yelled angrily, Abraham turned around and looked out the back window as the horrific scene grew farther and farther away.

There were a few body's lying on the ground as well as one of the cars from their entourage and some of the aggressors were running after them still shooting, so perhaps the other men grabbed the merchandise before fleeing.

"Jesus Christ" Ivan said still shaken up, rocking back and forth with his head resting in his hands.

Abraham's heart was still beating wildly, shaking the rest of his body. Michael stared at Ivan looking sick, as Ivan told him the events that had taken place earlier that day.

"...they were arguing with Nikolai about something and then they started firing and then one of the guys raised his gun in Abraham's direction so I ran up behind him and pulled him down. After that I guess our guys started shooting at them but the guys up front didn't stand a chance"

Everyone was gathered in Michael's office and the only other survivor was nursing his arm where he'd been shot running to the car.

"Everyone else had been killed or wounded too badly to run and God knows what they're going to go through. I don't think they were the guys we were supposed to meet."

"Why the hell didn't you do something about it then?" Michael shouted. "It could have been the feds for all you would have known!"

Ivan stared back at Michael shamefully. Michael massaged his temples and breathed heavily.

"Get me their CEO on the phone. I swear if they knew anything about this..." He finally said, muttering inaudibly near the end.

Ivan did so, getting a receptionist at first but then was immediately redirected to the CEO's office. He tapped his wrist projecting the noise from his phone into the room.

"Hello? Michael?" the voice said nervously.

"What the fuck happened! Did you have anything to do with this?" Michael screamed angrily.

"No, no Michael we didn't have anything to do with it, I promise. My guys had the shit beat out of them and were tied up in the cars that I sent. Someone fucked us both. I just found out about it because the police called me about my cars and men that were at the scene. I'm fucked; you have to talk to the mayor for me, please Michael. I'll give you anything if you get me out of this," he pleaded.

Michael stared off into the distance contemplating this new information.

"I'll see what I can do, but you'd better have your guys tell me exactly what happened and if you hear anything you tell me first!" Michael said disheartened at learning the situation, having hoped for a little more information.

"Hang up" Michael demanded. Ivan did so but kept his phone projected knowing what the next move would be. Michael stroked his graying hair back and said "get me Semion on the phone." Ivan did.

"Michael?" a deep voice answered.

"The deal got fucked. Someone knew everything," Michael said despairingly.

"I told you just to do the deal at your warehouse. The cops aren't gonna make a move against you. You just better remember that you still owe me my cut."

Michael scowled but knew better than to say anything. "Don't worry you'll get it, but can you help me find whoever did this."

"Michael whatever happened is your business and you'd better fix it. You'd better show me that you still have control."

Michael was filled with a mix of anger and fear, knowing that if he didn't fix this then his whole business was ruined.

"Don't worry I'll find them. If you hear anything please tell me though."

The line went dead.

"That mobster son of a bitch! Ivan, you and Abraham better get out there and find out who did this or were all fucked," Michael said angrily.

There was an awkward pause in the room as everyone thought.

"What are you waiting for, get the out there!" Michael yelled.

Abraham and Ivan were dropped off at the quaint little café where they'd been picked up earlier that morning after running all over town tracking down useless leads. The night had come out of nowhere and the streets were almost empty save for a couple of homeless and a few stragglers.

"I think I'm going to go clear my head, if you want to come?" Ivan asked obviously stressed out from searching for answers all day while barely knowing the questions.

Abraham knew what he meant by "go clear his head" but the fake love solicited by those types of women wasn't as tempting for Abraham. For Ivan it was an escape from reality. At the club he could find a love and sense of belonging that only lasted a couple of hours and with some alcohol it was believable enough.

"Sorry, I'm just going to head back, maybe stop and get something to eat," Abraham said looking off toward the apartment. He glanced back at Ivan. "Thanks though, for today. Pulling me down when the shooting started."

"No problem," Ivan laughed "It's been a long day. Guess I'll see you later then," he said clapping Abraham on the shoulder and with that he started walking back toward the café's direction.

Abraham watched him for a couple of seconds and then turned to go his way. No matter how hard he tried Abraham couldn't get the day's events out of his mind as he walked along the dark desolate street. It was disturbing really. This was the first time that anything had gone wrong since Abraham had started working for Michael and from the shaken way everyone else reacted to the news it had been a long time for everyone else as well. Michael had seemed so untouchable that the sudden mortality of the situation had been a shock. Who would try and upset the order of things. Michael paid the mob their cut and paid off anyone that could potentially put him out of business, but it was a huge city and they did most of their business in 3 or 4 districts, so it was possible that someone else was moving in on their turf, but if that were true then things would have been handled a little more civil, at first anyways. They were businessmen after all, not mobsters.

The street beside the sidewalk on which Abraham walked was abandoned, the only sign of life being the symmetrically scattered lamp posts, giving the street an eerie feel. The shrubbery on the bank in the middle of the street would occasionally sway in the wind and off in the distance there were various unrecognizable sounds from the sleeping city. He looked ahead, seeing the signs on the buildings glowing, some just words, others pictures. It had a sort of uneasy beauty about it from the lack of life, giving it a false identity. He walked on getting closer to his apartment building. He heard a noise behind him and turned his head just in time to step out of the way of a knife jabbing at him.

He grabbed the arm connected to the knife and held it away from himself, throwing the man against the alleyway wall he had just materialized from. He jabbed the hooded man in the face several times and beat his arm against the brick until he let go of the knife; the man letting out a scream of pain as Abraham did so. Abraham then threw the man over his hip, sending him crashing to the ground, and then Abraham dropped to his knee to continue. He pulled back his arm ready to deal the blow.

"Stop" the man gargled through his bloody mouth raising his left arm to beg Abraham to stop.

Abraham glared at him debating and trying to catch his breath. The man was almost young and had a sharp nose atop of a handsome face, which was only masked by the man's blood mixed tears, almost making it look as though he were crying blood. He was spitting blood up as he talked from whatever damage Abraham had done to the inside of his mouth. Abraham rose up off his knee and stood over the man calming himself down from the excitement, with clenched fists.

"Who are you" Abraham asked trying to regain his breath.

The man was cringing his eyes from the pain and momentarily opened them to stare Abraham in the eyes as he talked.

"You'd have best just let me kill you. Now fate's gonna intervene," the man threatened.

Abraham got back on a knee and grabbed the man's collar, pulling the man closer to himself.

"What are you talking about?" he demanded confused.

"One cannot learn if he does not pay attention. Maybe you'd have less questions then," the man said accusingly.

"What the hell are you talking about?" Abraham said again raising his voice and tightening his grip, although he started to feel worse in his stomach.

"You don't know do you? There are certain things that you've overlooked," the man said. "Everything's going to change. It's already in the process especially since today's events."

"Tell me what you know or I'll end you right fucking now!" Abraham yelled angrily, impatient with the man's games.

The man stared into Abraham's eyes, angrily and then finally said with an air of calm, "If you really want to find out what's going on then go to Johnny's .45 and ask for Vladamir Sergievich. He'll let tell you what you want to know, though it won't matter."

Abraham thought about trying to beat the information out of the man but he felt that the man would never talk or keep talking in riddles. He let the man's collar go and stood up; looking menacingly as he towered over the man's shaking broken body.

"If you try this again, I'll kill you," Abraham said coldly and then started towards his apartment again; looking over his back sporadically to make sure the man didn't try anything else.

The short walk back to Abraham's apartment was troubling and thoughts were running through his mind like a marathon, giving him no pleasure in the serenity of the night. Everything was cumulating in his mind. There was a lot more at play than Abraham had let himself believe, or better yet, he had let himself become too susceptible from trying to cope instead of using his head. He didn't know what was going on or how it involved him, but he was undeniably being left in the dark about a couple of things. Michael would have been furious if he'd known that Abraham let the man go, but if he ever wanted to get the answers he sought he'd have to postpone finding out who was trying to overthrow Michael. Resolution was coming and what it brought was a mystery.

Chapter 10

As the sun rose in the backdrop of the city, creating a blinding light as it reflected off the glass and metal, Abraham stood fully awake watching it, as he leaned against the wall of his room. It was a beautiful city. It had been pollution free for so many years now, having fully financed clean energy and more environmental friendly goods off the money that they would have had to spend on other services that a largely populated city simply could not do. The darkness of the night sky slowly changed into a more energetic light blue as the sun emerged, parting the sky into regions of blues oranges and yellows, as only a master of the sky can do. If Abraham's mind hadn't been so preoccupied he might have even enjoyed seeing this, but he had been awake long before it arrived and would be long after it was gone, and did not care for it as he had more consuming things on his mind than natural beauty. What had happened the previous night had left him in too agitated of a mood to get any sleep, so he had just lain in bed wishing for peace of mind, and eventually got up to look at the city as he thought. Whatever he was being kept in the dark about he was determined to find out. There was no question about whether or not he was going down to see the man who had been mentioned the night before and supposedly would have all the answers. Hopefully the man would be there, as early as it was, though it was doubtful, but there was no procrastination in Abraham's impatience. He looked at his watch; it was almost half past seven. It'd be past eight by the time he'd get to the bar anyways, so the place would be open, probably just cleaning up from the previous night, but they could tell him if they knew the man and where to find him.

Abraham walked all the way down to the bar, taking a rustic looking road, through a narrow ally, that had probably been there for a century and had vegetation growing on the sides as if it had been bordered by gardens at one point. Finally he came to the small bar that the man from the night before had spoken of. It had a sign out front beside the door with "Johnny's .45" lit up in a red light with the outline of a magnum pistol encasing the letters. It was an old bar, one like Abraham remembered from before prison. He pushed the ugly faded black door open and waked inside.

"We're closed" A man said from somewhere to the right.

Abraham looked around the dingy old place and spotted the source of the voice wiping down a table on the left of the entrance. There were several people still in the bar surprisingly, most likely regulars or friends of the establishment. One older man passed out in one of the booths, and another middle aged man sitting at the bar still drinking a half full glass of a golden brown liquid, and still yet another young blonde girl behind the bar cleaning foamy mugs in the sink. The place had old cracked wooden tables and a wooden floor but still maintained a dignified look about itself. It was slightly western themed, giving the name of the bar a bit of a credit.

"I'm looking for someone?" Abraham said turning and beginning to walk toward the man washing tables, whom he assumed was the owner.

The man suddenly had a look of recognition come over his face.

"Uhh… who is it your looking for," the man said cautiously.

"Vladamir Sergievich, do you know him?"

The man looked confused and quit scrubbing the table to stand up straighter, as to seem bigger and more intimidating but unfortunately for him he had a kind face with a large white beard and bulging belly, so that he looked more like St. Nick than someone to be careful with.

"Yea, what would a man like you want with him?"

"A man like me?" Abraham asked humorously offended and raising his eyebrows as to enforce his question.

"I meant no disrespect; it's just you work for Michael don't you?"

"Yeah?" Abraham said inquisitively still slowly walking toward the man.

"Well, all I meant was that Vlad doesn't really have much to do with things of that nature. He's a bit uptight of a man, comes here quite often and just drinks by himself. Kind of a sad man actually, but it's no surprise with what happened to his daughter," he said with a despairing tone looking back at the young lady washing the mugs.

"Do you know where I can find him then?"

"You're not going to hurt him are you? He's never done anything wrong or nothing."

"I'll be the judge of that. Just tell me where I can find him. And remember my reputation before you think about lying to me. I'd hate to have to come back here," Abraham said knowing full well that he wasn't going to do anything to the man, but even so the man bought his bluff.

"He lives a couple blocks away in an apartment complex called Afterworld I think and that's all I know about that," he said desperately.

Abraham nodded his head and walked out. He walked on down the old road in the direction the man had pointed, with his hands in his jacket pockets to keep them from getting cold in the chill of the morning, looking at the signs and more specifically for the ones advertising apartments. His phone started vibrating.

"Hello."

"Abraham where are you!" a rushed voice said.

"I'm walking back to the apartment. What's the matter; I was getting something to eat."

"Look, I found one of the slimy fucks from the deal. Get over here as fast as you can."

It was Ivan. He must have been looking all night.

"It's near the business district over on the Southside. I'll send the directions too you. You'll have to take a cab, sorry."

The line went dead and the conversation was over as fast as it had begun. He would have to deal with Vlad later, as intense as Ivan had sounded. Abraham called a taxi and read the directions Ivan had given him for the auto-drive. He was dropped off at a large cluster of old cheap buildings and in the backdrop of them were the gigantic skyscrapers of the business district where all the biggest companies in the country conducted business. The business district was by far one of the nicest parts of the town, and in comparison to where Abraham had been dropped off it was a bit ironic. There were large apartments around him with broken windows and patchy paint work. To the side of one of the complexes, metal, cloth, and wood came together to create small makeshift houses and built a kind of staircase onto one of the smaller apartment buildings. Lots of remnants of older buildings lay around as well and the larger apartments around the area kept the neighborhood in a constant shadow of darkness. Abraham walked up to the smaller apartment with the slum built onto it, and opened the old door. It was halfway broken and creaked loudly as he entered throwing out any chance of being discrete. It had probably been kicked in at one point by the police or whoever.

The inside of the building had slowly decayed through time. The walls were peeling, the floor was missing planks, and dirt and debris were everywhere. There were a couple of bony body's laying on the dirty hardwood floor as well, either asleep or dead it was hard to tell. He walked on watching his step. It looked as though a wind had come through destroying everything and everyone. In a city so beautiful it was hard to conceptualize that it had such a dark side. How could this have happened with all the money and resources the city had? It had been such a beautiful city but it was slowly showing its true form. He walked up the creaking stairs, scared that they would collapse under his weight, till he reached the third floor. He walked toward the hallways and as he turned to walk to the left he realized that the slums weren't just built against and on top of the building they were connected to it, covering up the truth that half the apartment had collapsed from faulty architecture. Up ahead of him the wooden floor of the apartment turned into the rusted metal of the slums. What had happened to the building that the right side of it had collapsed? He walked on through the slums. The wind screamed through the structure from the openings in the metal and Abraham felt as though the entire flimsy structure would collapse. He stepped over someone sitting against the wall of the slum, who didn't even bother to look at him and just sat there whispering to themselves and slightly convulsing. They looked half-dead. Their eyes were in the back of their skull and their nose was bleeding but they were breathing heavy enough through their drooling mouth to be able to tell they were alive.

He walked around a piece of the sheet metal sticking out as a kind of barrier between rooms and saw Ivan up ahead standing over a bleeding beaten man with his gun out. Ivan turned around when he heard Abraham coming.

"Finally" He said. "He knows someone that works for Michael that was involved but he isn't talking. Wanted you here in case I ran into trouble from some of these junkies"

"Okay."

Abraham understood and took his gun out of his belt, a little taken by his surroundings. Ivan was probably going to put the man within ten inches of his life in which case some of his junkie friends may try to help him out by stabbing Ivan in the back. If something did happen this wouldn't be the best place to be, since they were surrounded by junkies but it had to be done, at least in Ivan's mind. Ivan went over to the man and pointed his gun at his foot.

"I'm going to blow your foot off. And maybe if you tell me what I want to know I won't blow your other one off," he said coldly, pulling the trigger without even giving the man time to respond.

The shot went off and blood splattered the ground followed by a hysterical cry as if it were synchronized. The man started whimpering and flinching in pain, tears running down his filth covered face.

"Are you going to tell me?" Ivan said forcefully.

The man didn't say anything. Ivan savagely smashed the butt of his gun into the man's face, several times yelling pervasively at him.

"Are you feeling more talkative yet or am I going to have to blow your other foot off also!?" The man foolishly held strong.

Ivan put the gun to the man's remaining foot. As soon as he did, the man cried out and put his hands up as if they would protect him. He opened his mouth and tried speaking over the blood that was pouring out of his mouth. Abraham noticed that what teeth he had left were just barely hanging, making it even more difficult to talk.

"Tell me what I want to know!" Ivan shouted angrily at the man "Tell me!"

Abraham's attention suddenly was drawn to movement he saw from the way he'd come. He pointed his gun waiting for the skeletons in the doorway to make a move. They shied back, only flocking to the excitement to observe.

"I don know a ames!" the man said desperately through his crying and swollen mouth.

"hey me me at he aparmens call Sacifice roo eigh nie one. Plea, Plea on ill me," the man pleaded curling up into a ball afterward and crying hysterically.

Ivan backed off.

"I'd better not have to come back here," he threatened.

"Let's go," he said, holstering his gun in his belt and continuing to glare at the man.

They walked back down the way that Abraham had come up and as they passed the skeletons in the doorway Abraham watched his and Ivan's back making sure they weren't in trouble. Nothing would have happened even if Abraham hadn't watched out for them. The junkies just wanted a show and maybe even to loot the body if the man had been killed. It's an interesting thing the mind of a junkie. Man's worst attribute projected into an entire entity. Their consuming selfishness, all for a feeling of euphoria, provoking them to do all sorts of terrible things, which a normal person wouldn't ever even consider. Useless to the world, but still not at fault. What had happened in their lives to lead them to become so dependent most people will never understand. Abraham understood though and as they walked from the building he couldn't help feeling pity for them. He wasn't much for drugs, but having nearly gone crazy from his solitary confinement he understood trying to cope with the pain and anxiety that life brings. Ivan however had decided that they weren't strong enough people to deserve any better. They hurried into the car Ivan had taken there and began heading toward the apartment that the man had told them of. Ivan had a stern look on his strained his face. "It's not very far away. Just watch my back we may run into trouble here also." Abraham hadn't seen Ivan so dead serious and dedicated since that first time the morning after the nightclub. Michael must have really been getting to him lately, for him to be this stressed out.

They pulled up to a building in somewhat better condition than the one that they had previously been at, and once they got out they walked, almost ran, to the door and up the dusty wooden staircase. They came to the door eight hundred and ninety-one after so many flights of stairs. It was strange that someone would want to live on such a high floor, seeing as how the building looked as though it might collapse, but maybe the structure was better than Abraham had perceived, after all it had stood long enough to become as degraded as it was. Ivan kicked the door open and walked in, his gun raised, ready for anything, without even waiting for Abraham to get ready. Abraham followed him in, in such the same manner and scanned the room. It was surprising what they saw. Neither one of them had expected to walk into the aftermath of a massacre. Bodies' were scattered throughout the old apartment. Most of them looked no better than the junkies back at the slums, just dirty and malnourished. Broken glass was shattered all over the floor as well, and from all the bodies there were pools of blood covering the floor almost like paint, running down in drying streams to the sunken spots of the floor where it collected in pools. They had all been killed unsuspectingly being that most were unarmed. Ivan walked around in disbelief as did Abraham, checking faces as they went, not that they suspected to find anyone they knew. It was just something they were doing out of the disbelief of what they were witnessing. Seeing something so inhumane confounded them as to what to do. Abraham walked by one man who was lying sprawled out on one end of a couch. He looked like one of the scientists that Michael had working his lab.

"This guy look familiar?" he asked.

Ivan walked over cautiously so as to not get blood on his shoes.

"Yea, he's one of Michael's scientists. Or was, what the hell was he doing here?" Ivan asked to no one in particular. "I remember seeing a couple of these guys at the deal also. Let's get out of here. We'd better go tell Michael," he said not looking away from the dead scientist. The men turned around fast and walked out the door their thoughts following them like a disease. In less than fifteen minutes, they were standing in Michael's dreary office explaining where they'd come from. When they'd arrived Michael had been stressfully discussing business over the phone and as eager as he was to learn the news, none of it made him any happier.

"I get the feeling they knew we were looking around, so they tied up loose ends."

This weighed on Michael's mind, his anger surfacing over the betrayal of his employee.

"At least we know who betrayed us now. We just need to find out who's behind it," he said calmly. "Keep asking around, Semion hasn't called me back yet but I'm sure he's got someone looking."

Ivan nodded his head, staring at Michael curiously because of the odd way he was despondently gazing ahead of him at nothing in particular, lost in his own internal struggle.

"Wait" he said bringing the men to a halt as they began to head out the door. "Tomorrow nights the mayors re-election party so wear something nice and be their around nine, he'll want to meet the both of you. And Abraham, hold on for a little I need to talk to you."

Abraham hesitantly walked back in as Ivan left rejected, curious as to what Michael needed. As impossible as it was, Abraham began thinking of the incident from the night before. Michael gestured for Abraham to have a seat in one of the dark leather chairs sitting in front of his desk.

"How're things going for you?" Michael asked as he poured himself a drink from a decoratively designed glass bottle.

Abraham was taken aback, not expecting such an awkwardly causal question. "It's okay I guess. Why do you ask?"

"Good, just curious you know you don't talk too much, so I just wanted to make sure everything was alright," Michael answered, choking back a large swallow of the clear liquid.

Abraham nodded still curious as to what this was all about. Michael rubbed his eyes with his free hand.

"What about Ivan, he been acting strange lately or anything?"

"No not really, he's just been stressed trying to figure out what's been going on, like the rest of us."

"So you haven't been seeing him as much have you."

Abraham began to understand what Michael's intentions were.

"I guess not"

"Well let me know if he does anything out of the ordinary. I love my brother but he's not the most trustworthy guy," Michael said.

"Why do you say that?"

"Well with the reason he went to prison and all."

Abraham's confusion was clear on his face.

"He didn't tell you, did he?"

"He told me he was caught robbing a heroin dealer."

"There's more to it than that," Michael said. "There were three guys there, Ivan, Mark the man you guys killed, and our cousin Peter. They'd had everything under control and the robbery was going well but then the feds showed up because they were tracking the suppliers. The three of them ran but Mark was caught almost instantly. So it was only Ivan and Peter but the feds were closing in. Ivan decided that the only way for him to escape was to shoot Peter to slow the feds up. So he did...to our own cousin. He was caught anyways in the end. Peter died from his wound and Mark made a deal with the feds, so that's why Ivan went to that hell hole of a prison." Michael finished his story. "I love my brother but I don't trust him. If the time comes he will always do what benefits himself. Promise me you'll watch him, Abraham."

Abraham thought and nodded his head, taking in the information that he'd just been given.

"I will."

"Thanks Abraham. I'll see you tomorrow tonight"

Abraham nodded again and stood up to leave. Was this the version of the story that Mark was referring to as he was on his deathbed? Abraham couldn't be sure. As much as he wanted to believe he knew the story of what had actually occurred, none of the story's narrator's had revealed what happened without their own objectives at heart. Regardless of what happened it held no bearing over Abraham's life.

What bothered him was the dishonesty and deceit that was being inflicted upon him from seemingly everywhere. With time though, all things would become clear to him.

Chapter 11

Abraham stared at himself in the mirror feeling anxious about the party that night. He still felt like the walls were closing in on him when he was around a large group of people and tonight there would be plenty. Very rich men and women talking about politics and business, neither of which Abraham had any interest in. He tightened up his tie. He looked good; healthy even. It was hard to believe the man staring back at him was the same one from just a couple of months earlier. His hair had grown longer and thicker, as well as his muscles. They still held the same definition they had when he was in the prison but they were fuller now and didn't look quite so much like skin and bone. He combed his dark hair with a little black metal comb, making sure to dust off the dead hairs that fell like leaves from a tree about his suit jacket. Finishing up, he walked out into the living room and waited on Ivan. He changed the wall into a window to look out over the glowing city as the blanket of night held fast over it. His nerves were still stirring in his stomach as he thought of how the night would go; A long night of fake smiles, boring conversations, and intolerable people; such as it always is with the rich people of the world. The sight of the city put them to ease a little, as calm as it looked. He stared out into the sky hoping to see the moon but it was missing from the scene. Perhaps it was the lights of the city casting the backdrop of the sky into complete darkness, and perhaps the moon could no longer fight to remain a source of light over the city, as it and the city had so long struggled over. Ivan walked out.

How do I look?" He said, letting out a sigh of exhaustion and then smiling jokingly, and turning around in a circle as if to model. Abraham laughed. "You ready to go?"

"Yeah, I guess," Abraham said unenthusiastically.

"It won't be so bad. Just a lot of rich idiots talking about things they barely understand," Ivan said as they shut the door behind them and walked down to the street where their ride was waiting.

They were driven far out of the city from the time it seemed to take, and the miles of dark forest and shrubbery verified that notion. Finally they pulled up to a castle like mansion that Abraham could barely believe only one family lived in. The house had been built within the past 100 years by the mayor's executive grandfather and had a classical type of architecture to it that was almost extinct in that part of the world. The mayor's father had died recently from cancer and when the time came for the mayor to claim his inheritance he had married a trophy wife, and with her they had had one boy and one girl with perfectly selected gene's, making them the golden children of the city, but with that knowledge came a vast amount of pride that had corrupted their minds. As the car pulled up to the estate they were driven through 3 sets of gates connecting the grounds to the mansion, the passengers being scanned at every one of them, to make sure they weren't intruders. It was built on a majestic hill, that must have been a beautiful sight during the day with all the natural beauty surrounding it, and had a black marble staircase leading to the front door, and a large oak patio on the right side where people were sitting at tables, drinking and talking happily. The men stepped out of the car and were greeted by a servant, who showed them to the door after telling the car where to park. As they walked to the door Abraham took in the bushes of flowers on both sides of the stair, both rows sprouting little white flowers much the same as the trees that were planted scarcely around the grounds. The actual house was about five stories with tall pearly pillars enclosing the entrance, and was glowing with white lights all around the edges of the building to accentuate its grandness.

"You gentlemen are friends of Michaels, am I right?" the servant asked robotically.

"Yeah" Ivan said.

"If you'll go up to the second floor, then you'll find him and everyone else. Have a great evening," he said with an in-genuine smile and then quickly walked back to his post at the half-moon driveway.

They walked through the pillared entrance and into the lower party, seeing all of the high society people gathered, drinking fine alcohols and gossiping excitedly. All of them had on incredibly fancy clothes, dresses with diamonds in the design and gold earrings, gold dresses; pure crystals and gem stones were rampant among the women forming bands around their wrists and fingers, as well as other pieces of jewelry. The men all had on sleek black and white tuxedos, most with gold rings or watches made completely from diamonds or rubies or sapphires. Just from the accessories they had on they could probably have funded a war. Seeing all the precious stone made Abraham remember a book he'd read about a utopic society that made their toilets out of gold. It's odd how material wealth is based on something simply because it's shiny. It goes to show just how shallow humanity is as a race. The floors were pearly white as well as the walls with all the velvet black furniture scattered throughout, and blood red designs decorated the wall, with paintings and various other art. Large bodyguards were stationed all around, especially at the entrances to prevent anyone from overstepping where they weren't welcome. A magnificent Siberian tiger rug lay in the center of the common room, a couple of the drunken guests were already accidently stepping on the hide getting it dirty, not even having noticed. The mayor must be a hunter judging from all the animal heads hanging from the wall. Large exotic beasts were among them, even an extinct rhinoceros head hung at the center of the display, being his biggest game.

They began ascending the black winding staircase to where they were told Michael would be. Once they had climbed the stairs they saw much of the same as the first floor, just in more abundance and much more expensive looking alcohols and clothes. These parties must have cost thousands but with the mayor's unofficial income and embezzling it wasn't surprising that he could afford such an event. Ivan spotted Michael, as they walked around the groups of people, and they walked over to him. He was laughing and talking with a large group of people, looking to be the main focus of attention.

"Michael" Ivan shouted over the noise of the music trying to get his attention.

Michael looked over to see who had called his name and smiled happily that they were there.

"Alex, come here and meet my brother and our friend, Abraham," he said gesturing for a man to come over to him.

A path parted for Ivan and Abraham to walk over to Michael and as they did, a tall, slightly pudgy man, with a full head of slimy dark brown hair, walked over to Michael, glancing back and forth between Michael and the two of them as he drank a glass of golden champagne.

"This is Alex Gavrilov, the mayor of Yekaterinburg," Michael said laughing, though nothing was funny.

"This is my brother Ivan, and our friend Abraham," Michael said, finishing the introduction.

Abraham realized Michael was a little drunk from the slurring in his voice.

"Nice to meet you boys, always good to know who keeps my city afloat," Alex said, shaking each of their hands firmly.

"Well, I don't know if I'd say that" Ivan said half joking.

"Your brother's been one of my biggest campaign funders so I owe him a lot, as well as the both of you. The drinks are over there and there are plenty of women here as you can tell..." he said gesturing to the guests of the party smiling arrogantly. "If you guys need anything, don't hesitate to ask." It was funny the way he talked to them, unquestionably arrogant, but with a careful manner, choosing his words delicately.

Abraham and Ivan drank their fill of the sweet crystalline and gold colored drinks that were being carried around by young pretty waitresses in plain black dresses. They listened to rich pompous people talk about the economy and various other societal problems, as if they intended to do anything about them. Most were also just commonly repeated statements, as if they all had a shared brain that was diseased by a single narrow minded thought of splendor. After a while, Abraham had grown tired of hearing these types of conversations and walked out onto the balcony to get away from the noise. The night air's cool breeze gently brushed against his face and hair as he leaned against the railing. He pulled out a cigarette and cupped it to protect the flame from the wind as he lighted it. He stood there slowly smoking, exhaling the milky smoke and thinking about the skeletons from the day before, in that old disintegrating apartment building. The city was far off in the distance, but the light could be seen for kilometers through the darkness of night. The wild of the forests and plains captivated him, as natural beauty always had. He heard footsteps behind him and turned to see who it was; hoping that this wasn't someone he had come outside to escape from. It was the mayor's niece who'd been pointed out to him earlier along with the rest of the mayor's important family. She slyly walked out as though not to disturb Abraham. She was wearing a white glowing dress with a diamond necklace, and white gloves covering her hands. Her light brown hair was done up in a bun for the party. She was a naturally beautiful woman, glowing with the eloquence of a movie star. She walked over to him, careful not to overstep herself. Abraham became nervous and looked at her inquisitively as she was about to speak.

"You wouldn't happen to have a lighter would you?" she said smiling, after hesitating for a second.

"Sure" he said pulling the lighter from his pocket and lighting her cigarette for her.

She leaned over to catch the flame.

"Thanks" she said.

She walked closer to Abraham and slightly leaned on the railing as he was doing, and stared out over the earth with him.

"I've never seen you here before. You're one of Michael's friends right?" She questioned.

Abraham smiled. "Friend's a bit strong of word for what I'd call our relationship" he joked. "I just work for him."

She raised her eyebrows in acknowledgment and had a slight grin.

"Oh now I see. Your one of his thugs?" she said in a comical manner.

"I guess that's one way of putting it," Abraham said embarrassed at having been identified as a thug.

"We'll how would you put it then?" She said inquisitively with an air of mystery about the question.

"Just someone who's waiting for another opportunity."

She leaned in. "You get many of those in your line of work?"

"Not so far." Abraham shook his head, blowing smoke out and laughing.

"So how do you like the party?"

"Not really my type of thing," he said, his answer provoking her to smile.

"Well if it makes you feel better I'm only here because I have to be also. Being political royalty in this town does have its disadvantages."

Abraham smiled. "That would be pretty awful."

"Some days I can barely get myself out of bed," she said.

Abraham laughed at the thought. There was a silence between them but was enjoyable none the less. She began to say something, but was interrupted by Ivan who walked hastily out to Abraham.

"Hey Abraham, you ready to go? I'm done with this," he said obviously annoyed.

Abraham opened his mouth and then looked at the woman wanting to stay. Ivan realized that he'd interrupted, but didn't speak for embarrassment.

"It was nice to meet you," Abraham said staring into her blue eyes as if he was gazing across the ocean.

"You too Abraham" she said joking about having learned the answer to her interrupted question. Abraham smiled, turning away from her to leave.

"By the way, my names Alyona" Abraham paused and turned back to see her smile, and in turn an awkward smile lit up his face as he realized he had forgotten to ask.

He walked with Ivan back through the party in a dreamy state, paying just enough attention to maneuver his way through. Perhaps he was idealizing the encounter too much; he had been away from women quite a while, impairing his judgment between flirtation and friendly conversation.

"I'm sorry about that Abraham. I just couldn't take being there anymore," Ivan said apologetically.

"Don't worry about it. I was about ready to go," he lied.

On the way back to the apartment, Abraham's mind was far removed from reality, painting pictures of romance and epic love stories, letting them corrupt his mind. He was so caught up in his thoughts that he had barely comprehended their arrival and when he stepped to exit the car he stumbled foolishly. Ivan laughed at him and made a petty joke about him being drunk. Abraham laughed along, trying his best to keep in the present, instead of reliving the past hour.

The woman began to fade from his mind as he and Ivan hunted for more leads, over the next couple days, and it began to seem as though their meeting had only been an unconnected event in his life. Abraham and Ivan were sitting, eating dinner at the diner near their apartment as they did most nights. It wasn't bad food and was incomparable to the gruel they ate in the prison. Abraham was finishing up his steak when he felt his phone ringing. It wasn't a number he recognized, none of Michael's men or Michael himself had a number like that and it was odd that the caller ID had no name as it usually did. He showed Ivan thinking he might know, but he shook his head. Abraham touched the rectangle in the center of his wrist and brought his wrist up by his ear.

"Hello, Abraham," a woman's voice said.

"Hello, yes, who is this?" He asked suspiciously.

"It's Alyona, from the party the other night of course," she said as if he should have recognized her voice.

"Oh, hi how are you?" He said in surprise, as his stomach became uneasy.

"I'm fine, I was wondering if you were free tonight and wanted to meet me at this place in the old town. I know it's not the fanciest place to be seen but the interior is just gorgeous."

"Yea sure, that sounds great."

"Great! I'll send you the address and meet you there around 10, okay?" She said excitedly.

"Okay, see you there." Abraham laughed.

"Bye, bye now," she said hanging up.

Ivan was trying to contain himself but his emotions slowly won out. He removed his hand from his mouth and grinned knowingly.

"Looks like someone's got a date." Abraham laughed and shook his head at Ivan.

"Yeah." He laughed.

"Is it that temptress from the other night, you sly dog, you," Ivan said.

Abraham smiled, having been at a loss for words. He decided to change when they got back to the apartment, putting on a light blue shirt underneath his black jacket, with his black pants and dress shoes. He was nervous about seeing her again but he was equally as intrigued. When it was time he walked out to where he'd had the car wait for him and sat in the back. He was trying to control himself. He'd have a couple drinks and be fine. When he arrived, he saw it was a small little club, built out of a sandy white colored brick. A watery blue sign read "Ocean's Breeze" and hung obtrusively over the wide glass doors. As he walked into the dimly blue lit bar, the reason for the title was revealed. All the walls around him were fish tanks full of exotic fish swimming around playgrounds of castles and sunken boats. There were even sharks and squids in some of the bigger tanks. The blue lighting of the bar went well with the deep red carpeted floor and once he walked out of the entryway into the actual bar, the place opened up and the mural designed into the carpet was a beautiful image of the sea, with mermaids and wales and the mighty Greek God Poseidon at the center. He saw Alyona sitting at a small round table on the side, gazing at the sea turtles swimming majestically through the tank in front of her. The blue light of the tank was reflecting beautifully off of her porcelain white skin. She looked amazing. Her hair was done up in a bun again, like it was the other night, and she was wearing a short chrome dress that cut off at her thighs. She looked hypnotized by the caged animals, watching them swimming through the water, paying her no attention back. Abraham realized that he'd stopped moving and quickly collected himself, and began walking over to her. She looked over and smiled happily at his arrival, having noticed him as he drew nearer.

"Hi, how do you like it?" she asked him curiously as he sat down across from her.

"It's amazing, I've never been anywhere like this," Abraham replied.

"It's been here for years and I've just recently found out about it. It's so beautiful and I just love watching the fish in the tanks swimming around...." She talked on happily, just as Abraham was happy to listen to her, and would occasionally say something himself. The curious way she smiled at him and the way she glanced at him to make sure she wasn't boring him, was tearing him to pieces. He could barely think straight enough to keep the conversation going. She would pause occasionally and smile at him hoping desperately that he would say something, and then finally he would think of something and she would smile wide and laugh. The night felt like a drunken daze, nothing could have spoiled the evening. It seemed like only an hour had passed when they finally left the bar, saying goodnight to the fish, and walking out into the cold night. They walked slowly through the late hour, talking as if they'd long since been acquainted. For all Abraham could have known, the world around them had all but stopped. Nothing else needed to exist, because in this moment he was exactly where he wanted to be. The only thing that was real was her, which was ironic compared to how dream like the night had felt. If he could stay like this the rest of his life he would do anything, go anywhere, it didn't matter. If this was what death was like he could only wish for a shorter life. He wanted to stay in this moment, and from the way she looked and smiled at him he knew that she couldn't have felt any other way. After an hour of walking that seemed like seconds they arrived to her tall glassy apartment building, the nightlights reflecting off of it, making it seem as though it were a diamond palace. He looked into her eyes. There was such a sparkle of life in those sapphires, shining brighter than even the sun. He lifted his hand and brushed her hair back off her cheek and held the side of her head gently. She reached up and held his hand there. Abraham leaned in and kissed her. His nerves were making him a little jittery but it didn't show too much. As they passionately kissed, Abraham put his left arm around her as she put her other hand on the back of his head pulling him closer to her. She backed away to take a break and Abraham followed her up to her condo. They went in and lay on her black leather couch, holding each other in a loving embrace. Abraham was so overwhelmed with her, that he couldn't have even described the condo if his life depended on it. "I knew there was something different about you," she said gently stroking his cheek. Abraham was at a loss for words. Then finally he quietly said "I hope this isn't a dream." She pulled him close and whispered into his ear, "If it is then it's the best dream I've ever had."

Abraham woke the next morning lying in satin blue sheets next to Alyona, feeling more content and clear headed than he had felt in his fondest memories. He replayed the events from the night before over and over again in his mind, watching Alyona as she slept, with a subtle smile on his face, grateful that it wasn't just a dream. But all good things end and after a while his wrist band began vibrating on his piled clothes. It was Ivan with a message that Michael wanted to meet with them about setting up a deal. Abraham took a deep breath after half reading the message, annoyed that his time there had come to an end. He sat up in the bed, stirring Alyona as he did so.

"Good morning," she sleepily said, shyly smiling at him.

"Morning," Abraham said and leaned over to kiss her.

"I have to go."

"Already," she said puffing her lips out showing her disapproval.

"I'm sorry. I'll call you later," Abraham said and leaned in to kiss her one last time before getting out of bed to get dressed.

"I'll be waiting," she said sleepily.

Abraham looked back and smiled at her as he buttoned his shirt.

Chapter 12

Under a gray sky Abraham rode to a small medical facility near the center of town, nostalgically thinking of his past week with Alyona. Even Michael's agitation with him and Ivan could not distract him from the elated hopefulness that it had brought on. After sometime the car finally pulled up in front of the facility and Abraham jumped out carrying a briefcase, hurrying to complete the task in hopes that Michael would have nothing further for him to do that day. The facility was a small hospital that was mainly used by the surrounding poor lower class that inhabited the shabby areas around it. The facility itself wasn't in the best of conditions but the staff did the best they could to keep it from disintegrating into the conditions of the buildings around it. Abraham walked up the dirty concrete steps, eyeing the doorway as a young blonde girl in skimpy clothing impassively walked out. Her face was cut up and bruised but she had no shame of this as she attempted to ask Abraham what he was doing later. He passed her without thought and walked into the hospital as the glass doors automatically opened for him.

The inside of the hospital was as most hospitals are; Clean, stale, and filled with the ever-present feeling of death. There were several people waiting, all of which were poor miserable people, suffering from different ailments and addictions. Some even had children which provoked even more of a compassionate response. Abraham grimaced internally, revealing nothing through his body language. He walked up to the front desk where a young brunette woman sat filling out forms. She didn't look up even as Abraham stood in front of her.

"I'm here to see Dr. Larin on behalf of Michael Komarov," he said, clenching the silver briefcase in his hand tighter.

The young woman looked up in surprise but collected herself.

"Just a second," she said standing up and walking out the door of the small reception office.

A door to the left of Abraham opened and the woman was standing in the doorway.

"Right this way," she said.

Abraham followed the young woman down several hallways occasionally turning left or right. The facility was much bigger than its humble façade outside. As they walked Abraham could see into some of the rooms they passed, which were occupied by more of the same that he saw in the lobby. There were often more than three to a room as well and as small as the rooms were it was unpleasant to think of how overcrowded the facility was. Finally they came to a stop outside a door with a sign that read "Dr. Larin" on the outside. The woman knocked subtly but the doctor responded and the woman opened the door.

"This man's here to see you on Michael Komarov's behalf, Doctor"

"Thank you, Vera," the doctor said motioning for Abraham to step inside his office. Vera politely left, closing the door as she did so.

"Please, take a seat," the doctor said directing Abraham to the red leather chairs in front of his desk.

Abraham noted how clean and orderly the office was, thinking that the doctor must be somewhat responsible for the rest of the facilities appearance. The doctor himself was much older than Abraham, but still retained some youth in his features. He had gray hair, a strong jaw line, and deep green eyes that looked as though they could see into the very depths of one's soul. But his overall complexion was kind, so as there was nothing off putting about his demeanor and in turn provoked a desire for his friendship and approval.

"Dimitri," he said extending his hand.

Abraham took it, "Abraham."

"So Michael sent you."

"Yeah, he was wanting two-thousand rubbles for it," Abraham said setting the briefcase on the doctor's desk.

The doctor turned the briefcase to face himself and opened it. Inside where two, carefully packaged glass phials.

"Alright," he said closing the briefcase.

"Hell of a world we live. I pay two-thousand for these two and then have to turn around and sell them for twice as much or UCB will shut us down for attempting to violate the patent." As he spoke the doctor stood up and walked over to a locked fridge and began opening it.

"They not have as much of a problem with you buying them illegally to start with?" Abraham asked curiously.

"Surprisingly, no. They look the other way and don't try to get too involved in it as they actually make more money that way. Also it has a lot to do with class separation. Eugenics, genetics, it's all the same thing; just a reason to degrade someone and think of them as less of a human being than yourself." The doctor opened the locked fridge and pulled out a wad of money. He walked back over to Abraham and handed him the money.

"Well you can definitely see that looking at the patients here," Abraham said.

"My patients here are the forgotten people who are only brought up as a sort of pathos when a politician or company wants to make a small gain. Nothing is ever improved for them. Their addictions and joblessness go unaffected. This is the cost of success. One group of people have to be oppressed and thrown to the wolves for another to live comfortably," the doctor responded. Abraham nodded. "People have become so corrupted all due to what they've been told is the truth by media outlets. They sell themselves and everything they believe in for a misguided sense of happiness, the illusion of happiness really," the doctor continued. "But it won't change. Even if the government fell it would only be replaced by another regime. So I do what I can. Help the people who are doomed to suffer regardless of how hard they try to overcome it." Abraham stared at the doctor's thoughtful gaze, listening intently. The doctor smiled suddenly. "You know it's funny actually. As advanced and evolved as man is supposed to be with these genetics, it seems that he's no better than he was before. Man will be man."

"It's a shit story," Abraham replied smiling. The doctor subtly laughed.

"You're a very smart man doctor. "I'd better be going though," Abraham said earnestly as he stood up and pocketed the wad of money.

"It's been nice meeting you," the doctor said, standing to shake Abraham's hand one last time.

"You too," Abraham said in reply.

With that Abraham walked out of the office and on through the facility contemplating the doctor's words. On arriving back to Michael's delicate home, which was located close to his business, Abraham walked up the brick steps leading to the door and knocked. Michael had a large amount of land for a city home, giving him a gorgeous front and back yard, decorated with various kinds of shrubs and flower beds. He also had a rather large gated driveway which curved around his property in a half-moon sort of way. The door was answered by one of Michael's disturbingly emotionless servants. The silent despondent man held the door open as Abraham walked in into the foyer. Michael liked to have the appearance of being a cultured man without actually being one. He had modern art placed symmetrically around his home to the point of it being a bit distasteful. As Abraham walked through the foyer and into the living room he could hear the screaming coming from the study.

"You're useless! You'd be better off in that damn prison for all you've done for me! You can't find one person, one, that's got anything to do with this!"

As Abraham was walking into the study he passed Michael's quiet submissive wife, who at the moment had a face so beaten and bruised it could have been a boxer's. Abraham stared at her as he passed, surprised to see her so beaten, unable to understand what she might have done to deserve it seeing that she never spoke, at least in the time Abraham had known her. He walked into the study and found Michael agitated and out of breath leaning against a bookshelf. Ivan stood by the doorway looking hurt. Michael looked up when Abraham came in.

"You got my money," he demanded. Abraham pulled it out of his pocket to show him. "Well fucking say so." Michael walked greedily over to Abraham and snatched the money from Abraham's out stretch hand. "Good, Now I was telling this worthless bag of piss, that if you two don't find something out soon about whoever it is that's trying to put me out of business, then I'll..." Michael stuttered, his thought progress slowing from his weariness, "... I can't take no more of this is that understood!" he said glaring at Abraham and Ivan. "Good, now get out of here."

Abraham and Ivan left in a hurry, neither wanting to be around Michael. As they rode, Ivan stared at the ground. "He didn't mean any of that towards us. He's just upset at what all's going on." Abraham glanced at Ivan. "You wanna stop at the park real quick," Ivan asked. "Sure, what for?" Abraham asked curiously, staring at Ivan for a moment while he was waiting for an answer but when one didn't come, Abraham looked away. The car stopped at a quaint little park, scattered with tall trees and bushes. Abraham followed Ivan over to a bench on the side of the paved walkway. The two men sat down and stared off in silence.

"You know when we was kids Michael was always getting me out of trouble. After our parents died he looked after me. After the first time I went away something changed in him. He'd tried so hard to make things work that when they didn't I think he just reverted into himself, disappointed with the world. Ever since, no matter what he gets it's never enough. I know it seems like he's a selfish son-of a bitch but there's a different side to him. I hope it's still there at least." Abraham stared at the ground listening.

"Your brother loves you. Like you said he's just under a lot of pressure." Abraham wasn't sure he believed the words he said, but said them nonetheless.

"Yeah," Ivan said under his breath.

The chilly wind picked up causing the trees to sway more as if in a dance. As if by reaction Ivan's mood suddenly lifted.

"I ever tell you bout my son." Ivan smiled.

"No," Abraham said taken aback, having been under the opposite impression.

"Well I had him with some girl in my twenties. I don't really remember the girl that well because she took off and left me with the boy but the little guy was just like me anyways. I loved that kid but I couldn't have taken care of him. I ended up leaving him at an orphanage one day." The wind increased gently for a moment as Ivan spoke. "Wish I could see him now. See what he became, had to be something more than what I am." Ivan stared at the ground, deep in thought as the two men sat there. Abraham searched for something comforting to say but the like many times the words never come when you need them most. "Let's get out of here," Ivan said. The two men slowly stood up and walked back to the car. As sorry as Abraham felt for Ivan he couldn't help but think of Alyona and what giving her up would mean, just as Ivan had his son.

Chapter 13

It was hard for Abraham to concentrate on things the next couple weeks. Now that he had been seeing Alyona, his job had begun to weigh more on him. He thought more often about the lives he was ripping apart and everything else that he'd done for Michael since arriving in Yekaterinburg. It wasn't worth it anymore. Alyona had given him more than he'd ever hoped for, and the possibility of being happy again after so long was too important to let it fall apart because of the uncertainty and deceit surrounding him. Michael's demeanor had only been getting worse and more unpredictable as well. He was starting to resemble Ahab, chasing a ghost of his obsession, having Ivan and Abraham going all over the town to interrogate and kill people he vaguely suspected. He'd already been having his own employees followed and harassed. Abraham figured it was only a matter of time before Michael began to suspect him.

Today they were traveling halfway across town to a broken down little apartment complex near one of the small rivers that ran through Yekaterinburg. The skyline was almost beautiful as they rode, with the sun falling beneath the skyscrapers adding to their tremendous shadows, which had already swallowed the greater east side of the town. The actual apartment just faded into the background of the spectacle. It had a tannish brown exterior, with plenty of chips and boarded up windows, and the inside wasn't much better, but it was still in nicer condition than some of the others in the city. As they entered, Abraham looked over the apartment, but only saw the man that Ivan had went straight for and begun beating and demanding what the man owed Michael. Abraham proceeded to lean against the lavender wall of the apartment, from which he didn't plan on leaving until they were done there.

He stared mindlessly at Ivan, not paying much attention to what he was doing, but at the same time trying to look as if was he was to avoid trouble. Thoughts ran through his mind as if they were running a marathon. He thought about leaving with Alyona and living in some remote town, like the one he and Ivan had stayed at before coming to Yekaterinburg. It was a nice town; rustic, welcoming, charming rather in a way. He could live there and get a job somewhere, as long as Alyona was with him he would be fine. But what if she didn't want to go, he asked himself, thinking about the reality of what that would bring. It would be hard for her to leave her family, though she never has much good to say about them. While Abraham was busy thinking, Ivan was working.

"It's not my problem that Michael wants his money now. Maybe he said he gave you another week, or maybe he didn't, either way he wants it now!" Ivan yelled furiously, trying to make the man understand.

Ivan may not have liked doing the job, but he was born for it. He just blocked most of the feelings out and saw it as business. Once he stopped seeing them as independent people with families, the job became much easier for him.

"Please, please just give me another week. I don't get paid till next Friday, and I can barely make ends meet as…"

Ivan cut him off. "I don't want to hear your sob story," he said pulling out his gun and pointing at the kneeling man's head, prepared for an execution.

The man had only had his eyes tearing because of the pain that Ivan had caused him, but this new development brought him to hysterical crying and begging. Ivan heard something to his back left and turned quickly around to see what was going on. Abraham had been so lost in thought that he'd barely noticed the tall, dark figure dart out of the closet in front of him. Had he been a second late he would have had a knife stuck in his throat, but as luck would have it, he dodged to the right just in time for the knife to only slice his shoulder. In his attempt to evade the knife he tripped over his feet in the sudden shock of the situation, falling to the hard dusty wood floor. He lifted his head almost immediately, though only to see the man burst blood from his chest after Ivan shot him, spraying Abraham who lay on the floor in front of him. The man fell to his knees as his eyes rolled back and his head began bobbing. Ivan must have hit his heart. Abraham was alarmed but when the man fell on him getting blood all over his clothes, it turned to disgust, and he quickly got out from under the man, jumping to his feet still shocked and feeling ashamed.

"What's wrong with you? Pay attention! You're supposed to have my back," Ivan said, frowning at Abraham in confusion.

"Sorry," Abraham said quietly in disbelief, through heavy breaths holding his injured shoulder.

Ivan looked back at the man kneeling in front of him.

"Now why didn't you tell us there was a man in the closet? Were you planning on us being killed?" Ivan asked, playing with the man's emotions.

Abraham looked back at the body of the man, who'd died just seconds before. He was young. Maybe a teenager even, it was hard to tell because of how dirty the man was, masking most of his prominent features in grime. He felt sick seeing so much blood, which scared him. He hadn't felt like this in all his time working with Ivan until that moment. His mind had so refused with what he was doing that it was causing his body to feel sick. He had to make a change; that he was now certain of.

"...now if you don't pay by next week, that'll be you, don't think you can runaway either. We'll find you!" Ivan said pointing at the body in front of Abraham as an example. "Let's go" He said to Abraham, as he turned and walked out the door.

"What's been up with you? Lately you seem to be so distant. Does it have something to do with that girl you've been seeing?" Ivan asked as they walked, concerned that Abraham had almost been killed.

"No, she doesn't have anything to do with it," Abraham said immediately defending her.

They were hurrying down the street getting further and further away from the apartment they had just been at. They began hearing police sirens ringing out over the wind and noise of the city.

"I just have been thinking a lot, mainly about Michael. You don't think he'd start to suspect me do you?"

"What? No of course not. He did ask but I put at him at ease. You don't have anything to worry about," Ivan said, quickly responding to settle Abraham's mind. "He's just going through a lot of stress right now because of what all's going on. When this is all over, things will go back to the way they were before. Trust me you've got nothing to worry about."

"Thanks," Abraham said looking unconvinced. Ivan saw it but was at a loss for words as to what else he could say to comfort him.

"I think I'm going to go see Alyona though. Just give me a call if something comes up."

"Really? Well okay, I'll see you later," Ivan said worried. Abraham nodded and started to cross the desolate street. Ivan watched him as he went, trying to understand what was troubling Abraham.

It was past dusk as Abraham walked to Alyona's condo. It was a couple miles away, but he decided to walk through the city and give himself time to think. When he finally arrived it was dark out, but seemed even livelier than when it was day because of the music and lights. Alyona had lived in a small condo for a couple of years, never really wanting to move any closer or further away from all the nightlife. It was a little nicer than Abrahams but the only visual difference was that the doors opened as you came close to them, scanning your face in the database of residents and visitors. Alyona had entered Abraham in the system, so the door to the lounge knew to let him. It was those kinds of small differences that made her condo incredibly more expensive than Abrahams. People pay for anything that made life more uninvolved it seemed.

"Hey," Abraham said kissing her.

"Hello," she said grinning as she let him into her apartment, but then noticing the blood stained shirt beneath his jacket as he passed, she immediately gasped, her eyes growing wide. "Are you hurt?" she said, covering her mouth with her hand.

"Oh sorry, my shoulders just cut a little. I'm sorry, I completely forgot about that," he said, surprised that he'd been so lost in thought as to forget his wound. She looked at him confused as to how he could have forgotten that he had blood on his clothes as well as a knife wound, though it was true; it had completely escaped his mind.

"I just walked through the city like this, I'm such an idiot." Abraham laughed at himself in disbelief, looking down at his clothes and bringing his hand up to massage his temples.

"Did you kill someone?" she said with her mouth still covered.

"No, Ivan did, I'm so sorry, I wouldn't have come if I'd realized."

She shook her head. "Come in and I'll wash them for you."

He walked in to the condo out of the doorway and began to take off the stained clothes.

"What were you guys doing?" she asked irritated for no reason and then upon seeing the knife wound, clasped her hands to her mouth again, as if she were preventing herself from screaming. "Oh dear!" she exclaimed sadly.

"I'm fine really, it's not that deep. Ivan was just getting some guy to pay up and I wasn't paying attention and some guy jumped out of the closet with a knife. Ivan shot him and that's how all this happened," he said, gesturing to his clothes. He looked at his arm. It looked worse than it felt. She shook her head and collected the clothes to wash.

"Have a seat and I'll go get you some healing patches," she said hastily. Abraham walked over to the couch and sat down. She didn't much care for looking out at the city as Abraham did, often having her holographic blinds set so that she was looking out over the ocean or a grassy meadow. She had grown up here after all, rendering the city as unimpressive. She would much prefer to look at the stars of the Milky Way. She came back and sat down beside him with her legs crossed on the couch, and began applying the patch. Abraham looked into her face as she carefully applied the patch smoothing the edges out. She noticed him staring and lifted her head from what she was doing for a quick kiss before returning her attention to the patch. "Be more careful," she said.

Abraham smiled.

"Okay you'll be all healed up in a couple of hours," she said repositioning herself so that her feet were off to the side of her and she was resting her head against Abrahams shoulder.

"You're going to get yourself killed," she said sadly.

Abraham stared at his feet clenching and then unclenching his jaw. "I was actually thinking about leaving." She looked up at him curiously.

"I've been thinking about leaving town for good," he said hoping that she would put it together. He turned to look at her.

"And going where?" she asked interested.

"I don't know; somewhere else, somewhere smaller," he said careful not to say too much.

"Why? You could just find another job and stop working for Michael."

"I don't think that would work." Abraham smiled at her childish ignorance. "Michael wouldn't let me do that, especially now with what's been going on. He's been getting scary lately, more unpredictable and paranoid. I figure if I don't leave soon then I might end up in a position that I don't want to be in," Abraham said, adding more drama than needed in hopes that she would be more sympathetic.

"What if we both just left?" she asked, finally asking what Abraham had been hoping for. "We could both just leave and start a new life somewhere else. I've lived here my entire life and things aren't going to get better for anyone. It's just as well that we leave all this behind. We could move somewhere near the ocean," she said. It was a romantics dream. Traveling the world together, getting away from society and the rest of the corrupt system of civilization. "Just give me a couple of weeks to get ready. I'll prepare everything, you just stay alive!" she said half-joking.

She knew that Abraham's answer was yes and always would be. She was smarter than she let Abraham know. They often played house watching TV, reading magazines, cooking a late supper together, enjoying each other's company. They joked and played with each other, hardly having much serious conversation or thoughts, just being happy in the moment. It was like that tonight and she fell asleep on the couch, lying on Abraham as they watched TV. It was some science show that Abraham hardly understood. He didn't even know the simplest terms that were being thrown around. It was late at night and the day before had caught up with Abraham, causing him to be more drowsy than he'd expected to be. Ivan would want him to be up early though, so he couldn't stay and sleep with Alyona tonight. He tried to get up without waking her but inevitably failed. She slowly opened her eyes yawning.

"Are you leaving?" she asked pouting her lip, as she usually did when Abraham was called away from being with her.

"Yeah, Ivan will want me up early with him to go check on some things. Sorry," he whispered, kissing her on the forehead, and then seeing her head rise up, kissing her soft lips. "Goodnight," Abraham whispered, standing up to leave. Before doing so he went to her bedroom and picked her up a blanket to cover herself up with. Half asleep she whispered

"thanks baby, I love you." He smiled and walked out of the apartment quietly.

Whether it was just the sleep talking or not, she'd said she loved him and he believed it. He loved her as well. She was the only redeeming thing in his life. He quickly walked back to his apartment happily thinking the entire way about them leaving together. After a while of walking he felt his wrist vibrate and he stopped dead in his tracks realizing the caller. The Id said, Vladimir Sergiviech. He stared at it, having forgotten about the whole thing over the past months.

"Hello," he answered cautiously.

"...Abraham," a deep voice asked. "I hear you're looking for me?"

Abraham didn't say anything.

"I have some information you may be interested in learning. Meet me at the Crossroads nightclub and we'll talk," the voice said hanging up.

Abraham frowned in fearful confusion as to what the man might tell him. He started desperately looking for a cab. He finally hailed one and jumped inside, his heart racing with his mind as he anxiously waited to arrive at the nightclub. What information did this man have? As little good as it did, he asked himself questions repetitively coming to conclusions and then dismissing them as ridiculous. He would only find out what this was about when he got there, but the anticipation was killing him. He had to be ready for anything. Half of him even suspected that he was being set up, but there was no stopping him if there was even a chance that he might learn some of the answers to his questions. Finally the cab pulled up to the club. It was in the same type of location where Alyona's apartment was but on the other side of the district, and the beat of the music from the other clubs still rattled him to the core. He ran inside of the nightclub, ignoring the line outside, but luckily the guards knew who he was and let him in. He rushed in, being immersed in a sudden bluish-darkness, and then a strobe light began blinking, lighting up the club sporadically in beat with the intensifying music. The man hadn't told Abraham anything about where he would be or what he looked like, making Abraham feel more unnerved about the situation. It had to be a trap he realized, but an unexplainable curiosity was preventing him from leaving. Adrenaline filled him, heightening his senses. He walked around aimlessly; looking for someone that he had no clue what they even looked like. It wasn't a very big club but it was plenty crowded, making it hard to see any sign of something out of the ordinary. The more he looked for it, the more he saw it though. People from all over the club were looking at him, some even whispering. He had to leave, now. He turned and began rushing out of the door when he saw a man in the corner undeniably staring at him. When he caught Abraham's attention, he lazily lifted his hand motioning for Abraham to come over. Abraham was catching his breath, embarrassed from his false paranoia, as he started walking over to the man, still hesitant about the man's intentions. He wiped the sweat off his forehead and then pulled his suit jacket tighter, collecting himself. He tried to get a better look at the man as he walked closer, but it was difficult with the lighting of the club. The man was older maybe in his late 50's judging by the graying brown hair and somewhat wrinkled face. He wore an old worn brown suit, which stood out among the rest of the clubs occupants. Abraham took a seat across the table in the booth that the man was sitting in. They sat there staring at each other, Abrahams more of a confused glare than the others.

"I hear you have something to tell me?" Abraham demanded.

"You've been working for a man named Michael have you not?" the man asked, irritating Abraham.

"You know who I am, don't play games."

"My apologies, I just thought I'd let you in on a secret, because word around is that you have no clue what you're even involved in."

The man was enjoying his superiority in the conversation.

"You see, I was a customer of his once. I bought muscle enhancing genes for my daughter to make her stronger, because, you see, she had weak legs from a rare birth defect; a mutation in her genes. Anyways, I paid off my debts in full, no problems... But unfortunately my daughter was diagnosed with cancer a few months later. So, most would consider it an unfortunate loss. I, however, stricken by grief..." he said overly dramatic. "Couldn't possibly understand why my daughter had been taken from me. I began searching for any possible thing that might have contributed to her death trying to find something to blame, but I came up empty handed in all my leads. In the end I decided to see if by some chance it was the genes that Michael had sold me, which was a dangerous accusation of course, so I covered it up by saying that I needed some more of them for myself. I had a biologist look the genes over and what he found was that, whenever the gene was spliced with a strand of DNA, the cell housing it began making thousands of copies of itself." Abraham didn't know what he meant, but the way he said it only made him more curious. "What that means, Abraham, is that the genes that I had bought and injected my own daughter with gave her a fast acting cancer. I killed my own daughter because of Michael's faulty product," he said angrily, glaring at Abraham passionately. Abraham could feel the man's pain in his words. He relaxed. "The only reason no one's caught on to this, is because most of his genes don't kill the host."

The two men sat there for a while in silence.

"I'm sorry about your daughter," Abraham said sincerely, not understanding what this had to do with him. "But is that all?"

"No there's one more thing. I just thought you might like to know the harm you're indirectly causing," Vladimir said taking a drink of the brown liquid in front of him.

"Do you know why Michael has such a great relationship with the mayor? I'll give you a hint; it's not because of all the money that Michael bribes him with." As the men stared at each other, Abraham desperately searched for the answer, hoping that he could find it so that Vladimir would have no surprise in store for him, but no answer came. "He sells people to the mayor," Vladimir said triumphantly as

Abraham's heart sank. "Yes," he laughed, "Michael sells people in his outfit, so...Michael never gets caught and the mayor gets votes because it looks like he's cleaning up crime throughout the city. Makes it look like he's doing a good job, you know."

Abraham was having a hard time processing this new information.

"How do you know this? ...Why are you telling me?" he blurted out half thinking.

"Like I said, I did quite a bit of research on him after my daughter passed, and because I want you to kill him. No one can get as close to him as you can and you're basically a ghost as far as the law is concerned. I can pay any price you want," Vladimir said desperately.

Everything was clear to Abraham now. It was Vladimir that was crippling Michael's deals. He was trying to ruin Michael and now he wanted Abraham to kill him, all for the revenge of his daughter.

"You must want to do something else with your life besides being a hired gun." Abraham thought of Alyona then and the lure of the money that Vladimir was offering. But doing this would be difficult and there was always Ivan to consider. He sat there for a few more moments thinking as Vladimir stared at Abraham, eagerly waiting for an answer.

"If that's all…" Abraham said deep in thought, as he stood to leave.

A confused frown came across the man's face. He had obviously expected a different answer, or at least had hoped for one. Abraham turned around and rushed out of the nightclub in a nightmare like haze as the blood rushed to his head. Michael was an informant. Abraham couldn't believe it, but thinking about Michael's relationship with the mayor, it made sense. Once he'd gotten outside he called Ivan to find out where Michael was.

"Hello?" Ivan answered drunk, unaware of the situation.

"Where's Michael?" Abraham demanded aggressively.

"Whoa what's wrong? Me and Mike are at the 365 club. Where are..."

Abraham hung up and angrily rushed to the 365 nightclub, one thought poisoning his mind as he went. Hatred was emitting from him to where people could almost tell, bystanders quickly removing themselves from his path. He'd never trusted Michael, but how could Ivan have kept all that information from him. He walked on only making himself angrier with every negative thought, unable to even stop and think about whether or not Ivan knew. Finally he arrived there after what seemed like hours and hurried all the way up to where they would be. Ivan jumped hastily to his feet to meet him away from the guests they were entertaining in their half-moon booth. Michael was slower, but lazily got to his feet as well, obviously unconcerned.

"You're an informant," Abraham yelled, angrily looking at Michael.

"Hey!" Michael yelled and hurried over to him, trying to silence him and hoping nobody had heard.

"Is that true?" Abraham demanded

"Come on Abraham, it's okay, we were going to tell you," Ivan said trying to calm him down.

"Look, it's a necessary part of business Abraham, or we'd all be locked up," Michael quickly whispered to Abraham.

"Abraham, Abraham, we're sorry, we just weren't sure how you'd take it, and we were planning on telling you, I promise you that," Ivan said.

"Does anyone know about me?" Abraham demanded.

"No, I promise, nobody knows nothing," Michael said desperately, trying to keep Abraham from yelling again.

Abraham shook his head and turned to leave.

"Hey come on Abraham we can work this out. Everything's okay!" Ivan begged.

Abraham didn't look back as he stormed out trying to clear his head but unable to do so. He walked for what seemed days angrily thinking about the betrayal. He'd decided not to tell Ivan or Michael about Vladimir but even so Michael would want to know how he found out that information. The man had lost his daughter because of Michael, so as far as Abraham was concerned he could have whatever justice he thought was necessary. Abraham was leaving soon with Alyona and that would be the end of it all for him. He would only be there for a couple more weeks. He just had to make it through them and then he would be in another town far away, just Alyona and him.

Chapter 14

Abraham sat shirtless on his bed staring out over the town as the sun rose from beyond the far side of the globe. He stared out over the buildings trying to get a glimpse of the world beyond the city but it was all engulfing, as if to suggest there was no world beyond. As great as the city had seemed, he'd grown weary of it. Knowing the foundations the city was built on and the repulsive creatures that inhabited it, had taken the glamor away from it, and led Abraham to the realization that just because something has an outward lure doesn't mean that it holds anything of value. Waiting for the week to finish out would be difficult, as anxious as he was to leave the city after the events of the week before, but Alyona insisted that she needed it. He had decided not to tell Alyona anything that he'd learned for her safety, in case Michael tried to find out what she knew. He had already asked Abraham how he'd found out, to which Abraham had responded that he'd learned it from some junkie while he was tracking down leads. Abraham desperately hoped that Michael believed him, but he knew better than to assume Michael was that susceptible. The tiles of the floor were cold against his feet. He closed his eyes and pretended he was back in his cell before any of this. No people, no city, nothing; Just himself, lonely, and maddening, slipping blissfully into the abyss. He wondered if he would have died by now if he'd stayed. There was something beautiful about madness, having no thoughts to cross your empty mind; just staring, waiting to die. His wrist started vibrating. It was Ivan. He answered, but hesitated to speak.

"Hello?" Ivan asked carefully, his guilt still weighing on him.

"Hey," Abraham said gradually.

"Hey, we're all set to go make the sell. We'll send a car to pick you up." He paused, contemplating his next words carefully. "You know were sorry. Michael just didn't want you to know if you didn't need to. I'm sorry Abraham; I would've told you if I'd known that things would be like this," Ivan said apologetically.

"It's fine; I just don't like feeling like I'm being kept in the dark."

"I'm sorry; we'll see you in a bit." With that Ivan hung up as did Abraham.

Abraham stood to his feet and finished getting dressed, watching himself in the mirror as he did so. He looked tired from the last few sleepless nights, the stress showing clearly on his face. At least this would be the last major deal he would be involved with. They'd been planning it for weeks, developing enough merchandise for the corporation that would be buying it, and it was going to be such a big payoff that Michael himself was going along out of respect. Abraham met the car and headed over to Michael's cluster of warehouses where they were making the sell at.

It was over on the south side of town, with some abandoned industrial buildings that had been purposely neglected after their usefulness had been fulfilled. The rust from the buildings was intense, giving the area a brownish hue, matching the sandy malnourished soil perfectly. Ivan and Michael were already there, accompanied by ten or so men. When Michael was explaining how the deal was going to be made a few weeks ago in his office, Abraham had thought it would take place inside one of his warehouses, but as his car pulled up he realized that he was wrong and they were doing it out in the open. When his car stopped, he stepped out and walked over to where Ivan was; kicking up the dusty light brown dirt with every step he took. "Hey," Ivan said as he saw Abraham walking up toward them. Michael turned and gave Abraham an acknowledging gesture with his hand; he was more preoccupied talking to one of his other men.

"The buyers will be here soon," Ivan said encouragingly, and almost on queue, a couple of small black cars pulled up twenty feet in front of them. "Or now," Ivan said laughing at the irony of his statement. As the new arrivals departed from their vehicles, Abraham noticed that there were ten or so of them as well, almost all outfitted in black suits. They represented a corporation that was working on sending people to space, from what Michael had said. They wanted the best humans that could be manufactured and when it came to cost and variety Michael was the best choice around for genetics. Michael and five of his thugs carrying rectangle aluminum containers walked up to the men and began the transaction.

Abraham hung back lazily. He looked around seeing how forgotten the industrial park had become, as it stood like a ghost town in the early day. Something caught Abraham's eyes in one of the windows though. The window was pretty dirty from dust and mud, and even cracked a little, but Abraham was almost certain he had seen a white blur pass through it from the other side. There was nothing like it in the others from what he could tell but it could have just been a fan or something. He thought he saw it move for a second time though. He squinted his eyes, trying to get a better glimpse of it in the morning sun.

Without a sound the glass suddenly broke revealing a man behind it, but before Abraham could really get a glimpse of him, a loud commotion took place off in front of him. He turned his head to see one of the business men slowly stumbling to the ground holding his neck as blood streamed from it. There was a lot of yelling that Abraham couldn't make out, but his adrenaline started pumping through his veins as he realized something was wrong, and in the confusion the businessmen's guards pulled out guns apprehensively. Abraham quickly pulled out the pistol he'd tucked into the back of his belt and pointed it at the men, changing targets trying to make sure he shot before one of them did. His heart was racing and sending all the blood to his head, only adding to his confusion, feeling the need to act without the knowledge of what to do. Everyone was shouting in fear trying to figure out what had happened, but then in the blink of an eye one of the businessman's head exploded, spraying one of his colleges with warm blood, and then there was no more talk. Michael was shot almost instantly, being so close, cringing his eyes in pain as the bullet buried itself deep in his shoulder, and dropping to his knees. His bodyguards surrounded him trying to protect their employer but the occasional one would fall down having been slain. Dust was kicked up as men ran in fear, trying to survive the confusion of the fire-fight. Abraham aimed and shot at the business men and then occasionally glanced back at the window to see if the instigator was still there, but he saw no one. Bullets hit the area around him kicking up the dust into his face. He dove to the ground by the car and took a knee, using the vehicle for cover. Michael had gotten back to the car as well and jumped inside as soon as he could, not bothering to leave the door open for anyone else.

"Abraham, let's go!" Ivan yelled frantically from somewhere to his right.

Abraham looked when he thought it was safe, and just in time to see Ivan take a bullet to his right chest cavity. Paralyzing shock took hold of Abraham, seeing his only friend the last few months die before him. He sat behind the vehicle for what felt like hours, as bullets buried into the car behind him and flew all around his feet, but Abraham was staring at Ivan in a trance, as he slowly made his way to the ground, the life steadily leaving him from the very moment he'd been shot. Suddenly the mirror on the passenger side shattered, sending glass flying at Abraham's face, bringing him back to reality. He ran over to his friend and pulled him through the battle back behind the car to safety as bullets rained down upon them. Abraham set Ivan up against the wheel and kneeled beside him trying hard to do something that would prolong Ivan's life. He was losing a lot of blood from his chest, as well as coughing plenty up since the bullet had penetrated the lung.

"Abraham," he managed out through the blood, taking Abraham's hand away from his bleeding chest as if to say it was no use trying to clot the blood.

"I'm sorry." He coughed.

"It's okay," Abraham said on the verge of tears, as Ivan slowly drifted away.

He opened his mouth to speak, but closed it and nodded instead, staring deep into Abraham's eyes reaching for his soul. He shook uncontrollably from the pain but as tears ran down his cheek, mixing with the blood as they went, Abraham could feel what Ivan no longer had the words to say. Abraham could no longer contain himself and slow tears began forming and running down his cheeks. He stared back into Ivan's eyes, his head burning with emotion as Ivan lost his grip on the world.

"Goodbye, my brother," Abraham said through shaky sobs.

Ivan glared into Abraham's eyes, with regret, love, and fear as he drifted away from the world. Abraham watched the light leave Ivan's glossy, hazel eyes and felt the shaking stop as Ivan went limp. Abraham balled up his fist and put it to his mouth as if to stop himself from screaming, and rolled over to sit against the car with Ivan's body. With his free hand he reached up and closed Ivan's eyes out of respect. Abraham sat for a few moments as it settled in that Ivan was dead. The back door beside him swung open and he could see that Michael had kicked it ajar.

"Get in!" he yelled, and Abraham stood up and rushed into the car saying goodbye to Ivan forever.

"What happened?" he asked hurt, after seeing Ivan's motionless corpse.

"He's dead," Abraham said unemotionally, wiping his face of the blood and tears, as police sirens finally became known to him, regardless of how long they had been sounding before.

Michael looked at his fallen brother sadly, his head lowering with guilt. They rode in silence the majority of the way back, both of them thinking about Ivan and Michael trying to clot the blood streaming from his wound. After a while, Abraham began feeling a threatening anxiety, as Michael's disgusted gaze burned through him. Abraham looked up to meet his eyes, as if questioning the reason.

"This is all your god damn fault," Michael said darkly accusing him.

"What?" Abraham asked confused.

"I know you're behind all this. I gave you everything and this is how you repay me!" he yelled angrily.

Abraham was taken aback by the realization of what Michael was thinking.

"You've been playing me for a fool this whole time; laughing behind my back with that whore!"

"Michael I'm not behind this, why would I put myself in that much danger if I was…"

Michael cut him off. "My brother and I brought you in, gave you a place to stay, a job, and then you go behind my back and try to put me out of business! You killed the only family I had left!"

Abraham shook his head in disbelief, trying to think of what he could say to make Michael listen to reason.

"You'll rot in hell, you spineless son of a bitch!" Michael yelled.

Slowly Michael's scowl turned into a contemptuous sneer as the men sat staring at one another.

"I did sell you out. Right after this deal was done the police were going to be waiting for you at your apartment. I wasn't going to say anything, but now I think I'd rather take the pleasure in telling you how fucked you are."

Abraham stared at Michael, panicking; wondering what was going to happen to him.

"I'd have figured you out sooner if it hadn't been for Ivan. He was just too stupid to realize your true nature and he died because of it," Michael said. "I guess it's fair though. You took the only person in this world that I love and I'm doing the same to you. Not that you yourself have long to live anyways."

"What are you talking about?" Abraham said, fearful of what Michael might say.

"I'm having that bitch killed as we speak. She'll be raped and beat and beg for death before my men will give it to her. Do you see what happens when you try and double cross me!" he yelled angrily as his faced strained.

"She had nothing to do with any of this!" Abraham screamed furiously.

"Don't lie to me, you cock roach. I know you two were conspiring against me. Spending all that time together and you didn't think I would find out what you were up too!" Michael screamed back.

Abraham quickly pulled his gun out.

"Where is she?" he asked as they drew close to Michael's building.

"What the hell...?" Michael said, his attention being drawn outside. Abraham looked and saw at least a dozen police units waiting for them.

"Auto-pilot, go to my house!" Michael anxiously shouted to the car.

The vehicle began changing its direction but the police had seen them and began chasing after them, their sirens blaring.

"Alex you double crossing..." Michael yelled angrily confused.

Abraham couldn't believe what was happening, but there was only one thought that guided him. He rose up and beat Michael relentlessly with the butt of his gun.

"Where is she!" he yelled, stopping the battery so that Michael could speak.

"What's the difference you won't be able to get to her?" Michael breathed in heavily, with a look of defeat as he realized the truth.

"She'll be at her condo, or whatever's left of her after those vicious fucks I sent rip her apart." Michael laughed through his bloodying face, still taking satisfaction in the pain it caused. Abraham hesitated for a second calming himself down, then pulled the trigger spraying the side and back window red. He felt nothing for Michael as he looked on his dead corpse, except perhaps vindication. He didn't care whether or not the police caught him, he just had to make sure that Alyona was alright, praying that she had been away from home when the men arrived. He looked out the windows nervously, getting a better idea of his surroundings and trying intensely to figure something out. The police would undoubtedly shut the car off remotely and if he didn't do something before that, then Alyona would die. The auto-pilot was driving him up the on-ramp onto the highway. This would be his only chance to escape, because once he was on the highway it was over. The buildings right beneath the on-ramp were barely close enough for him to jump onto and the fall not be fatal. He hoped at least. This would be his only chance. He opened the door, feeling the wind whipping him as the car gained speed. Suddenly he felt the car die. They police had shut it off. It was now or never. He jumped, barely clearing the side railing of the ramp, and flew through the air from the speed of the car. He felt the force of gravity pushing him back to earth and the wind resisting him. Fear gripped his entire being, realizing that there was no possible way of controlling himself as he descended back to earth. Finally he hit the roof of the building, rolling almost to the edge. His whole body was a nerve of pain, especially in his knees. He scrunched his face screaming in agony, but he recovered quickly, stumbling to his feet and limping, as he ran to the fire escape on the north side of the building. He quickly slid down it not bothering to climb each individual step. However he was unable to catch himself at the bottom from his weakened state and collapsed on cement, causing himself even more pain. He persevered though, standing back up and running to the street, one thought controlling his every movement. He limped around to the front of one of the parked cars and pulled out his gun to break the window. Abraham unlocked the door through the shattered window and slid into the car, and began to disable the autopilot. The engine roared as he pushed on the gas pedal and drove off toward Alyona's apartment, trying not to think of anything but the directions he had to take. He ran traffic lights, barely making it through the intersections, not even thinking to look and see if the police had caught up with him, because the car had undoubtedly sent an alarm to the department once

Abraham had stolen it. Finally after what felt like hours he arrived to her condo and jumped out of the vehicle, not even completely stopping the car. He ran up to her apartment the best he could with his injured legs. Abraham heard a muffled crying coming from the condo as he drew near and fearing the worst he burst in through the door, his heart pounding in fear and eyes wide in shock of what he thought he had been too late to prevent. He saw her tied up, laying on the ground and two of Michael's thugs spread out across the living room, surprised to see him, as they prepared an assortment of knives for their atrocities. He darted up to one of them and smacked him in the throat with his gun and pointed and shot at the further one, sending a mist of blood onto the wall from the man's gut. The man stumbled backward and fell against the wall, making a stain as he slid down it. Abraham turned back toward the other man without a thought, and began ferociously hitting his skull against the wall with his gun, denting the man's skull as he let his aggression out on him. The man finally slid down the wall either knocked out or dead, but regardless Abraham pointed his gun down at the man's head and squeezed the trigger. Dropping his gun to the ground he ran over to Alyona and kneeled down gently taking the gag out of her mouth and releasing her from the bindings. She was hysterically crying from the trauma, jumping up to embrace him as soon as she'd been freed.

"It's okay, I'm here, I'm here," Abraham reassured her, breathing more evenly now that he had her safe in his arms. "Everything's okay now."

"What's happening?" she cried with confusion in her voice.

"It's okay. You have to leave town. I took care of Michael, but it's not safe here anymore for you."

"Why are you telling me this? You're coming with me?" she asked staring into Abrahams eyes.

Abraham didn't say anything. He looked down sadly knowing the answer and trying to catch his breath.

"Abraham, say you're coming with me," she said, worried and starting to realize what Abraham meant to happen.

He looked back up into her eyes tearing up.

"I love you," he said trying to memorize her face knowing that this would be last time he would ever see her.

She looked at him trying to understand and beginning to cry more at the horrific realization of what would happen, and as she did so the police stormed in from the doorway yanking Abraham away and restraining Alyona as she tried to resist and hold onto Abraham. She struggled with great strength, but the police were too many for her, pulling her back and attempting to take her into another room. They beat Abrahams face until he submitted, falling to the ground. He felt blood trickling down the side of his face, as he tried to see through his beaten eyes. They yanked his arms back, tearing one out of its socket, and cuffed them together. Abraham felt the pain only half-heartedly, feeling more at peace having saved Alyona. He looked up to see her one last time as the police took her away to another room. She was reaching out trying to hold on to him and keep him with her, though it was useless. Her tears ran down her face, making it glimmer with the sun protruding through the window, making her look angelic. Abraham stared at her as long as he could but then he felt something sting him in the back and fluid entering into him. He began to feel a paralyzing drowsiness but fought it, trying to hold onto his last moments with Alyona. His vision began blurring and finally everything went black.

Chapter 15

It'd been days since Abraham had awoken to find himself in a solitary cell, similar to his old one. He'd taken a lifelong walk to the same exact spot it seemed. The wounds that the police had caused him hadn't been treated, nor had he received any sort of sustenance, but neither were on his mind as he wondered if Alyona was safe and prepared himself for what was to happen next. He had been having visions from the blood loss and hunger, often ones of Ivan or Alyona, but not happy ones. Terrifying ones that made him scream in agony, more so than the decaying way he felt. Tears streaked his bloodied dirty cheeks and as he looked up at the single beam of light that burst through a crack in his cell amidst the darkness, he hoped that she was okay.

His cell door opened creaking as it did so; surprising Abraham that he had a visitor. A tall dark figure walked in, the slight gleam of jewels reflecting from his attire.

"So... Abraham isn't it? Michael told me all about you, as well as his own brother. Poor choice trusting him on your part." It was the mayor, Alex, Abraham realized as the cloud of smoking protruding from his cigar cleared.

"Can't trust a guy like that. And when one of his own guys comes to me offering to give me a bigger cut with Michael out of the picture, I couldn't resist," he said emphasizing the last part and walking around confidently.

Abraham thought back to Vladimir; he must have had nothing to do with it after all.

"Anyway that was a nice little charade you put on saving my niece. And my gratitude, however our laws are strict and when my own family helps escaped convicts, they must be enforced. Can't have my niece running around with the likes of you, can I. No, she met her end, and you won't be far behind."

At that Abraham's heart dropped and he felt tears swelling up. He was overwhelmed with anger, but in his crippled state, his body refused to rise as much as he willed it.

"Not like we even have to bury you. You're already declared missing anyways, so it's a bit like you don't even exist. Well anyways, just thought I'd stop by and pay a visit."

He was taking a sadistic comfort in watching Abraham's quiet suffering. He left slowly, savoring the moment and grinning menacingly. Abraham stared at the floor crying softly now that he had privacy. He couldn't take living a second longer knowing that Alyona had been killed. Why should he wait for his death, for the comfort he hoped to find in the afterlife, and even more so he didn't want to give the mayor the satisfaction of an execution.

He bit his tongue hard producing blood, but he kept clenching his jaw tighter against his skull. He turned to lie on his back and choked as his body fought against him. Abraham closed his eyes finally in pain, after holding them open and watering so badly that his vision blurred. Through the pain he thought of Alyona, giving him the strength he needed. No thoughts crossed his mind as he slowly faded through the intense pain and suddenly there was a blinding white light.